ROUGH NIGHT
IN SLEEPING CAT

Kittredge felt the gun plucked from his holster; he heard it clatter to the floor. He bent forward, trying to throw his assailant over his head. At once the other two came closing in; one slammed at Kittredge's jaw with a fist; another planted a heavy boot in his stomach.

He went down, writhing in pain and cursing himself for his cocksure carelessness. All three were upon him, striking and kicking. He fought back at them, knowing the futility of fighting against such odds but wanting to get in a few licks. He struggled to his feet, only to be borne down by the sheer weight of the three. Flame exploded in his brain, and blackness came after it; his last consciousness was of Telford leaning forward in his chair watching all this, an intent look on his face, an eagerness in his eyes.

ROUGHSHOD

Norman A. Fox

A DELL BOOK

For Mother and Dad Spaulding

Published by
DELL PUBLISHING CO., INC.
1 Dag Hammarskjold Plaza
New York, New York 10017

For information, address Dodd, Mead & Company, Inc.
79 Madison Avenue, New York, New York 10016.
Dell ® TM 681510, Dell Publishing Co., Inc.

ISBN: 0-440-17518-6

Reprinted by arrangement with
Dodd, Mead & Company, Inc.
New York, New York
Printed in the United States of America
Previous Dell Edition #7518
New Dell Edition
First printing—February 1979

Chapter One: THE STAGE TO SLEEPING CAT

KITTREDGE FIRST SAW THE WOMAN before a stage station somewhere north of the Yellowstone; she was
a brightness against the drab setting of the square
stone building with its pole-and-earth roof; she stood
braced against the constant wind, and her figure
showed lithe and full-bodied with her clothes thus
molded against her. Kittredge was at once alert.
He was a virile man with virile appetites, and this
woman whetted a hunger made from the lonely
miles up out of Wyoming and all the long loneliness
that had been his life. But women had no place in
his scheme of things, and he told himself that his
stirred interest was only curiosity. The driver, whose
lofty perch he'd shared on this last hitch with the
Concord mud wagon rattling empty beneath them,
had said they might pick up passengers as well as a
change of horses at this station; for here the north-
south road crossed with the looping ruts that followed the Yellowstone upriver from Miles City.
Kittredge just hadn't expected a woman.

Viewed from the coach as they came swinging into the station, she was statuesque, tall in a cloak of
navy blue that unfurled to the wind. Kittredge had
a hasty glimpse of yellow, high-piled hair and a face
that struck him as handsome rather than beautiful.

Her trunk was beside her, an ancient portmanteau scarred by travel; that trunk told him much. When the coach squealed to a stop and he stiffly dismounted, he saw at once that the woman was older than he'd presumed, thirty, perhaps, and her face held a harshness. This was a land where women were likely to be of one of two kinds; and he thought then that he had her pegged, and was disappointed. Still, he touched his sombrero brim, and this brought to her eyes an inward smiling.

"You're an hour late," she said.

He looked along the east-west road. The dust of the stage which had fetched her this far had long since settled. He said, "We wouldn't be if I'd done the driving."

Her interest became marked; and her appraisal was frank, taking in his dusty garb, his belted six-shooter, his high stand. Such interest was more than feminine. He had the feeling that he was being judged as a horse might be judged by a prospective purchaser, and this aroused a resentment that stiffened his face. He could be a soft-spoken man or a blunt one, and he said gruffly, "I'm Reb Kittredge out of Texas by way of Buffalo, Wyoming. I'm bound for Sleeping Cat."

Her eyes ceased smiling. "I didn't ask."

"Now you won't have to," he said.

Behind him the stock tender was busy at changing the horses; he could hear the slap of leather and, from the corner of his eye, catch the swift, certain movements of the man. The driver with whom he'd ridden from Crow country, an old man mummified by too many seasons of handling the ribbons, brushed past him into the station, muttering about this being a chance to eat. Kittredge had tired of the swing stations' eternal bread and bacon, and the strong tea without sugar and milk which was called slumgullion; but he moved past the woman and bobbed under the doorway into the dim interior. He had the feeling that her eyes followed him, and he was already regretting his brusqueness. He had been born to a kinship with those who traveled rocky roads.

This station was like all the others on this traverse, scantily furnished and ill kept. Kittredge looked about him and had no appetite. He saw that they would have an additional passenger, for a man was here, morosely finishing a meal. Seated, this man gave the appearance of being tall; he was a slender one in his late twenties, dark-clad and wearing a dark wisp of a mustache. He might have been a gambler; his garb befitted one; his face was long and sensitive, and his fingers were long and tapering. But Kittredge at once spied the black case of a physician on the bench beside him. This man interested him as a species apart from his own.

The ancient driver was peering in the semigloom. "If it ain't Doc Farrell! Doc, it can't be more than two weeks since I hauled you this far south."

"It's been long enough," Farrell said.

"How's things in Miles?"

"The town's still standing." Farrell looked down at his plate and made of this gesture something that closed out the driver, leaving only the echo of the old man's vociferousness in the room.

Kittredge said to the driver, "Do we have to wait here?"

"Not unless you aim to eat."

"I can stand it to Sleeping Cat if you can."

The driver said, "I'll see if them horses are harnessed."

Ten minutes later they were ready to leave. The woman's trunk had been pitched into the rear boot together with a mail pouch that had been dropped off by the east-west stage. The driver climbed to his perch and inclined his head at Kittredge, but Kittredge shrugged, electing to ride inside. The woman and the morose Dr. Farrell had already installed themselves upon the rear seat; and though there was room for three, Kittredge took the forward seat and thus faced them. The driver's whip cracked, the oldster letting out a high, lifting yell; the coach lurched, and they were on their way northward.

They made a silent threesome inside the coach. The woman sat with her hands calmly folded in her lap; her gaze, when it touched Kittredge, held no animosity. He had the feeling that she had dismissed him, not caring about him one way or another. Farrell, his medicine kit between his feet, seemed always a man lost in thought; there was a dark, brooding look to him that spoke of an oppressive experience all too recent, and this interested Kittredge for a while. Farrell, he judged, looked always inward.

The constant swaying of the coach on its heavy leathers gave a hammocklike effect that soon lulled the travelers into a lethargy. The sun of late summer hammered upon the coach, and dust rose and found its way inside, and sometimes the woman coughed. Farrell was aroused by this; he gave her a sympathetic side glance and murmured something that was lost in the rattle of wheels. A kind man and a soft one, Kittredge decided.

The landscape was undergoing another change. After the hills of Wyoming, there had been rolling plains to the breaks of the Yellowstone, a land studded by sage and wild rose and blue lupine, with pine and stout juniper showing on the lifted rimrocks. Thus had Kittredge first seen Montana. Now the country ran flatter, so wide and lonesome as to put an ache in a man; and mountains stood to the far west, hazy and ethereal above the prairie. After an endlessness of this, the road began to climb; timber showed more frequently, and the far horizons were gone. Huge rock piles littered this land, sandstone heaps molded by wind and rain into weird shapes. Kittredge amused himself by finding faces in the rocks. Wild currant and gooseberry showed, and forget-me-nots on tall stalks.

The deeper they drove into this country, the thicker the timber became, and the rock heaps. Kittredge could understand why the lighter mud wagon, built closer to the ground than the larger mail coach, was used on this run.

The afternoon was more than half gone when they toiled to the top of a rise and the stage pulled to a stop in the shadow of one of the sandstone piles.

"Breathin' the horses," the driver said, coming down from his perch. "Anybody want a drink, there's a crick yonder."

Kittredge heard the music of the stream in the unexpected silence of stopped wheels. Farrell looked politely at the woman; she shook her head. Kittredge swung open the door and came to the ground, glad for its solid feel. His legs felt like stumps, but he moved swiftly, heading around the rocks and finding his way through brush toward the creek. It was a good two hundred yards from the road, and he felt the pull of exertion on his ankles and the needle-like crawl of sweat upon his back before he reached the stream.

He lowered himself and drank long, then looked at his reflection in the water. He said softly, "You're certainly a fine specimen of the handiwork of God," and roiled the water with his hand.

Standing, he had a moment while he listened to the talk of water over rocks, not really hearing it. He was detached from all the world in this isolation of brush and stream and sky; he was a man halfway from hither to thither, looking behind and ahead at the same time and not liking the looks of either. He had known these moments of self-appraisal before and found in them a deep-hidden discontent. He made a heavy shrug and closed his mind's eye against this inward peering. He was a surly man as he turned away from the creek.

Working toward the road; he moved silently through the brush, for this was habit with him. He came to a dead stop before he'd reached the rocks. He could not have named the warning that was keen as any yell; he had long followed a trade that had whetted him to the small signs, and it might have been that a blue jay stopped its raucous noisemaking or that the wind brought some small shard of sound that fitted no expected pattern. He only knew that he had been alerted to danger, and he strained his ears until he heard a voice from around the rock pile.

It was no voice belonging to the driver or Doc Farrell or the woman; it had a tone to it that rasped against Kittredge. He looked up at the pitted sandstone rearing above him, put his boot to it, and began climbing.

He was cautious about this, and silent. He attained a dozen feet and looked over the crest of the rock at the coach below him. He could see its flat roof and the railing around the outer edge. Backed against the coach, the two passengers stood with hands lifted, the driver beside them, his mummified face showing an old man's impotent anger. Three men sat saddles directly below Kittredge, their broad backs turned to him. They wore range garb, these three, and held guns in their hands; and one of them said in the harsh voice that had first caught Kittredge's attention, "You can dig deeper than that, I think. Get that ring off your finger, Doc!"

At Farrell's feet lay his watch and wallet. His face made a white smear in the sunlight, and he said in an agonized voice, "It's my wedding ring!"

"Get it off!"

Farrell lowered his hands to strip the ring from his finger; he tussled with it, then laid the ring carefully upon the wallet. He said in a strangled voice,

"Bring it back to me at Sleeping Cat and I'll pay you any price for it."

The holdup man who'd spoken swung his gun barrel toward the woman. "Now you," he said. "Shell out."

She was a cool one with none of the driver's anger showing, and none of Farrell's fear. She said, "I'm carrying nothing of value."

One of the other horsemen leaned forward in his saddle with an avidness made of more than greed. "She'll have jewelry; they always do. I saw her make a move toward the front of her dress when we rode up. She's hid something. I say let's strip her down." He giggled and started to lift himself out of the saddle, and Kittredge went into action then.

He already had his gun in his hand and he shook out a shot, not at those broad backs below him but at Dr. Farrell. Farrell had fallen into a crouch; his shoulders were hunched, and his face was a wild man's. He was set to launch himself at the three; but Kittredge's shot, plucking at his sleeve, straightened him and stiffened him. He looked up and thus was the first to see Kittredge, and his face showed disbelief.

Kittredge was shouting at the three horsemen, "Up with them!" Each moved as though jerked by the same string, half turning to see him. Two dropped their guns. One man was slow at raising his hands, and Kittredge's gun spoke again. A bright-red spot blossomed on the back of the gun hand of this one, and his gun fell. He howled in pain, but his hands went up.

The stage horses were prancing; and though a glance told Kittredge that the brake was set and the reins wrapped tightly, he was afraid the animals might bolt. He began clambering down the face of the rock; he felt his foot slip and jumped then, turning in the air as he jumped. He landed on his feet between two of the horsemen, but his gun was ready. He took two backward strides so he could command the trio and spoke to the driver over his shoulder.

"Know 'em?"

"The Jimson brothers. Used to work for one of the Sleeping Cat ranches. Got turned out for mavericking. That was two months ago. They've been hangin' around since. You remember them, Doc."

Farrell said, "I remember them."

Kittredge asked, "Farrell, did I draw blood on you?"

"No, but you ruined my coat." Anger gave a sharp edge to Farrell's voice. "Which side were you taking?"

Kittredge said, "Since you're not hurt, get out there and lift their guns."

"I'll do it," the woman said and quickly stepped forward and picked up the gun that had fallen from the wounded horseman's hand. She collected the other two as swiftly, being careful never to stand between Kittredge and the three. She was deft about this; and Kittredge's interest in her sharpened, admiration growing in him. The guns gathered, she stepped back to Kittredge's side and unloaded them, tossing the shells in one direction, the guns in another.

Kittredge looked at the three and saw that they were from a common mold. It was more than an obvious blood tie that made them alike; they were bearded, all, and solid-shouldered and thick of body; but it was the viciousness on them that was of a pattern. He had seen their kind on all the trails and in all the towns and held them in contempt.

"Get down," he ordered.

They dismounted and stood hating him with their eyes; and he said then, a grim humor in him, "Now mount again. Backward!"

One said, "Dammit—"

"Get at it!" Kittredge snapped and gestured with his gun.

They climbed aboard as Kittredge had directed. Kittredge said to nobody, "They've got saddle ropes. Put 'em to use."

He heard the throaty chuckle of the ancient driver, who moved forward and began lashing the three to their saddles. He was swift about this, and thorough. When he had finished, Kittredge said to the three hunched backs, "You're not worth wasting jail room on. Somebody will come across you and cut you loose and go and tell the tale. I hope you're laughed off this range."

One of the Jimsons said over his shoulder, "You'd be smarter to kill us, mister. Because we're sure as hell going to get you for this!"

Kittredge stepped forward, wrenching his sombrero free with his left hand. Moving among the horses, he swatted at their rumps and sent them galloping. They left the road and cut down a slope and disappeared into timber. Kittredge stood shaking with silent laughter.

"Best get going," the driver said.

Farrell had picked up his belongings and restored them. Into the stage again, Kittredge assumed his seat, and they lurched onward. Farrell sat twisting the wedding ring on his finger; Kittredge could feel the doctor's eyes on him; he could feel the man's animosity. Presently Kittredge said, "Doc, when they mentioned putting a hand on this girl, you went kind of crazy. You were set to jump armed men. It showed on you plain as day. There wasn't time to discourage you any other way, so I drove a shot at you. If I hadn't done it, you'd be dead now."

Farrell thought this over. "Perhaps that's right," he finally said, but his face still held sullen. "Do you do everything the roughshod way?"

Kittredge said, "I'm still alive." But his thought was that he had made Farrell look like a fool in front of the woman. Some men never forgave a thing like that.

The woman looked at Kittredge with that same careful appraisal she'd given him at the stage station, but it was to Farrell that she first spoke. "I am grateful for your attempted gallantry, Doctor. I shan't forget it." Then she said to Kittredge, "You handle a gun as though it were your business. I think you are just out of Johnson County."

"I mentioned Buffalo," Kittredge conceded.

She said, "My name is Cora Dufrayne. Yes, I know you didn't ask. I shall be living in Sleeping Cat. I hope to see you often, Mr. Kittredge."

Kittredge shrugged. "I go where my work takes me. I stay till it's done."

He closed his eyes then, a man wearied by heat and dust and the aftermath of excitement; and presently he dozed.

Chapter Two: LAST CHIP

CURLY MATHER FETCHED THE NEWS to his boss, coming into the Sleeping Cat hotel dining-room with his spurs jangling and crossing with an intent directness of purpose to where Dan Saxon took supper with his daughter Rita. Mather stood tall beside the table, a hard-muscled, weather-burned, youngish man with no laughter in him. Mather, Saxon thought, was the kind whose bearing foreshadowed what he would be when the years piled upon him; he showed an old man's earnestness in all things. There was a constant petulance to him, sharpened tonight by a sense of urgency that drew him wire-tight and made his voice challenging.

"Well," he announced, "he's here. Want to come and take a look at him?"

Dan Saxon smiled. He knew Mather in that closely inspected way an employer knows his top employee; he had found Mather to be one who gave a great intensity to the most trivial chore. Mostly this trait in Mather amused Saxon though sometimes it rubbed Saxon raw. Tonight he was amused. "Don't you suppose I heard the stage roll in, Curly?"

Mather held ramrod-stiff and said sourly, "I figgered you'd be interested." He added as an afterthought, "Doc Farrell came home on the same stage."

This brought a sardonic cast to Saxon's smile. "Now that's fitting and proper. One to cut a man down; another to patch him up." He toed out a chair, making of this a lazy gesture. "Sit down, Curly, and have a piece of pie. You can have any kind you want so long as it's dried apricot. Perhaps it will be the last Circle-S will ever buy you. Why should I care that Reb Kittredge has got to town? Telford's finished me off already. Kittredge won't even have to earn his pay."

He said this so calmly that Mather looked quickly at Rita Saxon as if seeking confirmation from her, Mather's eyes asking, *Is it so?* Rita had a sultry sadness to her tonight; she was a vibrant girl, olive-skinned and sloe-eyed and dark-haired as her Spanish mother had been; and she had the same liquid grace to her movements and the same promise of passion in her full lips. She had a way of stirring a man yet holding aloof from him; she had a smile that was both fire and ice. Mather looked at her and was at once hungry for her, forgetting everything else.

Dan Saxon, seeing this, said with faint irony, "She's the daughter of a busted rancher, Curly. Telford has picked up my notes from the bank. I learned that today. I got a wagonload of grub from Barney Shay, but he told me that the mercantile would have to see cash on the barrelhead from here on out. Next thing you know, Circle-S men will be on the Injun list at all the saloons. What is there left for this Reb Kittredge to do?"

Mather's lips thinned down, making his face ugly. His voice became harsher. "Then you've given up fighting?"

Saxon looked at him, seeing the recklessness in Mather's solid features, seeing the impatience, and Saxon sighed for years gone and youth lost. He felt a brief uncertainty, but he schooled his face against showing it. "No," he said. "There is one last fling in me—one more chip to be spent. I'll have a look at this Reb Kittredge."

He stood up from the table and was, as always, a living contradiction, a man with saddle swagger to his walk and the stamp of Montana's wind and rain and sun upon his long, aristocratic face; yet he favored a knee-length plantation-style coat and a string tie, and he wore his sombrero at the same rakish tilt he would have given a tall beaver. His hands were as long and tapering as Dr. Farrell's—gambler's hands. He was not a very tall man, yet he gave an impression of tallness. Something about him spoke of vast acres and cattle bred with meticulous care. Something about him flung the memory of older men back thirty years to Mississippi gambling-boats and Mississippi showboats. This anachronism was Dan Saxon.

He looked like a man with no more on his mind than an evening at cards or a few hours with old cronies discussing feed and the price of beef. On the threshold of disaster, he looked like that.

But Rita cried out suddenly, "Dad!"

Saxon's thought then was that she knew him— she knew him full well—and from her knowledge

came her fear. He was a softened man then. He had
raised her to face fear, to face all the realities of a
harsh way of life; but at this particular moment he
wanted to spare her. It might be his last charity, and
so he said, "I plan only to do whatever needs to be
done, Rita. Have another cup of coffee. I'll be back
before it has cooled."

He was aware that Curly Mather's gaze was hard
and steady and edged by a great curiosity, and he
could almost hear the unspoken question in Mather's
throat. This brought a secret amusement to Saxon;
his impulses often surprised Mather, and this last
one would hold the greatest surprise of all. He found
some perverse pleasure in this thought and, savoring
it, he crossed the clattersome dining-room to the
lobby, leaving Rita with Mather. He made it a point
to pause at the cashier's desk and buy a cigar, letting Rita see him do this. Then he moved beyond
her range of vision. Townsmen were filtering into
the lobby, and Saxon elbowed among these, past the
chairs where loiterers sat with their newspapers and
their idleness.

One of these looked up and said, "Good evening,
Dan."

Saxon said, "Good evening, Gault."

Gault Telford was a man running to flesh, a moon-
faced man whose face looked oddly proportioned, for
thick lenses enlarged his eyes, making them big and
startling. Those eyes held a glint of laughter; this
same hidden mirth twitched at the corners of his
lips, which were full and sensual and rubbery. Very
carefully he folded the newspaper and put it in his

suit-coat pocket and said mildly, "Are you of a mind to sell now, Dan?"

Saxon stripped the band from the cigar and gave Telford a soft smile. "And what would that add up to for me, once my notes were paid off?"

"A few thousand, Dan. I am not a haggling man. Nor am I a spiteful one. I don't wish to push you to the wall. Come around tomorrow and talk about it. Over a pint of beer and a good cigar. You need never have to fight a Montana winter again. There is St. Louis or San Antonio, or wherever your fancy may take you. A gentleman's cloth for you, Dan; a lady's life for your girl."

Saxon put away the unlighted cigar. "And all Sleeping Cat Basin one big syndicate of ranches with Gault Telford at their head."

"And you as my right hand, if you'd rather stay in Montana," Telford said. "I'd even retain your crew, down to the last man. You see, I am reasonable. We have known each other many years, my friend. Let's not have the ambition of either of us lay a shadow on our friendship."

Dan Saxon smiled again. "They tell me Reb Kittredge just climbed off the stage."

Something showed in Telford's magnified eyes, something feral that was at once gone. He spread his hands. "Sleeping Cat has become a tough town, Dan, with that railroad spur driving deeper into the hills every day. Count noses on the street and see how many construction crewmen are here spending their pay. Sleeping Cat is my town, and I want it an orderly town. That's why I sent for Kittredge.

You're jumping at shadows, Dan."

Saxon said, "Am I?" and still showed a faint amusement. "And for a solid month every bartender and hostler and roustabout has been telling me that Kittredge was coming. And laying bets as to the day and the hour. Why was that?" He was watching Telford closely, and his thought was that when you hit them in a soft spot, even the big ones grunted and began showing their teeth.

Telford shrugged. "When a man is a legend, Dan, people are bound to talk about him."

Saxon said, "I'll go see how broad this one is." He turned away from Telford and said over his shoulder, "No need to keep that beer on ice, Gault."

Walking out upon the hotel's railed porch, he paused at the head of the three steps leading down to the boardwalk. Diagonally across the way stood the stage station, logs silvered by weather. The Concord had now gone on to the wagon yard; and the crowd, drawn always by the excitement of its coming, had dispersed; and there was no man to be seen who held Dan Saxon's full interest. He peered hard and thought he saw movement just inside the station's shadowy doorway, and he waited then.

Sleeping Cat lay around him, two straggly rows of false fronts facing across a river of dust, a town born of cattle, a town born of chaos. The hitchracks were full, and at this twilight hour the lamps were just beginning to blossom. Cowboys rode in from the far reaches of the basin; the hills hemming the vast bowl of land were yonder shapes, vague in the dusk; and the wind that flowed down from them touched Sax-

on's cheek like a caress. Cowboys jangled their spurs
along the boardwalks; but the planking gave back,
also, the echo of the boots of railroad construction
workers, a new breed upon the land. Irish mostly,
those workers, with pantaloons tucked into high
boots and black handkerchiefs about their necks and
a great thirst possessing them. Sleeping Cat's popula-
tion had taken to tripling on railroad paydays.

Up the street a blast of sound came from the Bagdad, largest of the saloons, a first fanfare to launch
another night of revelry. Across the street Barney
Shay was rolling a barrel through the doorway of
his mercantile, while his clerk swept off the worn
wooden porch. Dan Saxon stood looking at Sleeping Cat, and he said softly, affectionately, "You're
an ugly old town."

Then Reb Kittredge shaped up in the doorway
of the stage office.

He looked like a man hard-driven by the winds
of chance, a man at once wolf-wary and wolf-wise.
There was dignity to him, the proud bearing of one
who had carved out his name in that Johnson County affair and a dozen lesser range wars and sent his
name before him and had now to walk erect in the
shadow of it. He was young—Saxon pegged him at
about twenty-five—but he was also old, old as the
hills, old as violence, old as Cain. He wore range
garb and carried a single gun belted low; his hat
was flat-brimmed and slanted above a face that was
gaunt and saturnine and held no cherished illusions.

He was Reb Kittredge, imported gunman. And
he was walking across the street toward the hotel

where Dan Saxon stood.

There was only a brief span of waiting, and yet it was long enough to send Saxon's memory rushing back across all the years—the river-boat years with their tinseled glory, the war years, the mavericking in Texas, the long trail north; the good years and the bad years; the accumulated years that had brought him to this night and this moment. He wondered then if all his living had been fashioned for this, if each turn of the trail had been meant to direct his footsteps to a given place at a given time. He wondered, and knew a certain regret, and a certain glory.

And then, strangely, looking at Reb Kittredge, he saw himself as he had been before those years had burdened him, young and lithe and proud, a hundred chips to be played, and life a heady game. So strong was this impression that when it faded he felt old and useless and spent, and was of a mind to turn back into the hotel. On a peopled street he felt lost and lonely, and the wind from the hills seemed to have turned cold.

Then he shrugged and came down to the boardwalk and moved a few paces along it until he was directly in line with Kittredge. Raising his voice, Saxon said, "That's just about far enough, friend."

Reb Kittredge stopped in the dust of midstreet, brought up short by the challenge. When he lifted his head, his nostrils flared in the manner of a fighting man, and all the slackness went out of his body; he was at once smelling trouble and readying himself for it. His eyes were blue and they measured

Saxon, and when he spoke, his voice showed a bridled temper. He said, "I don't recollect knowing you."

"The name doesn't matter. I'm the man you were fetched here to kill," Saxon said.

"Ah," Kittredge said and drew in a hard, full breath, his eyes showing a sharp wariness.

Saxon became conscious then of every small sound of the town, the distant voice of the summer wind in the cottonwoods, the clamor from the hotel, the stomping of a horse at a near-by hitchrail, the tinkle of the piano in the Bagdad. Someone close by said in an explosive gust of sound, "Kee-rist!" Saxon knew that men had paused in their striding, seeing here the shape of trouble and watching it out. The boot sole of the one who'd cursed scraped against the boardwalk as the man carefully removed himself to the shelter of a doorway.

Saxon brushed back the skirt of his long coat and exposed his gun, hooking a thumb close to it. He took a slaunchwise stand. "It might as well be here and now," he said.

Kittredge shook his head as though not believing this. "You're a damn fool."

"No, Kittredge. Just a man with one chip left."

Something crossed Kittredge's face that was made of both astonishment and impatience. His shoulders lifted and fell. "I've got no fight with you. Not yet."

Saxon said harshly, "Must I find words to make you fight? Is that it? Do you always have to pick the time and the place yourself? Maybe you want a high cutbank and your man with his back turned."

Kittredge's cheeks colored, and he took a spread-legged stand, his shoulders hunched slightly forward. His face turned blank; only his eyes were alive. "Start it!" he said.

Saxon made his move, his eyes holding tight on Kittredge, and in Saxon afterward was no true remembrance of how the rest came about. He knew that he got his own gun out of leather; he felt its weight in his hand and had a surety in that moment that he had bested Kittredge by the split second that made all the difference. He thought, *An old horse can still pull its load,* and was fiercely jubilant. Then gun thunder was in his ears, reverberating from the false fronts and filling the dusk; and pain was everywhere, running up from his hand and through him. His gun lay fallen in the dust at the boardwalk's edge; he stared at it. Kittredge stood with his own gun poised, smoke curling from it and lifting to the breeze and floating away.

Saxon looked down at his own right hand and saw that a long furrow had been raked across the back of it.

Kittredge came toward him and paused. His face was still blank, and he gave Saxon a look revealing nothing, neither compassion nor anger; but he said, "I could have shattered your wrist as easy. Don't ever prod me again. I hope you've got out of your craw whatever you had in it, mister."

Saxon said, "I should have remembered. Never take aces in another man's game."

Rita was there suddenly, come running out of the hotel, the high stand of Curly Mather looming behind her. Rita cried "Dad!" her voice both scared and angry. Mather gave Kittredge the fullness of his gaze and was an angry man come too late to vent his anger. Kittredge looked at Rita and lifted his hat and went on.

Saxon got a handkerchief from the breast pocket of his coat. "You'll have to help me, girl," he said.

She was calm, now that she'd found him alive. She wrapped the handkerchief around his bleeding hand. "Thank goodness Doc Farrell is back," she said. "We'll get you down to his place."

Men were coming now from doorways to go about their business; Sleeping Cat had had its violent moment, and only the ripples remained. Rita took Saxon's elbow and commenced steering him along the boardwalk, Mather hurrying to flank them, looking sour and troubled. To his foreman, Saxon said, "Go get the wagon hooked up and ride out with it. I'm staying in town tonight."

Mather's anger spilled over. "Are you hell-bent on getting yourself killed?"

Saxon said, "The cook's waiting on that grub. Do as I say!" He watched Mather go angling across the street, walking stiffly, his back a reproach. Saxon said, "He hasn't married Circle-S, not yet!"

Rita said, "Kittredge had forty years the best of you. Did you go crazy?"

"No," Saxon said. "I knew the edge was all his. I tried to offset those years by calling his hand when he was stiff from travel, and hungry, perhaps, and tired, and not yet expecting trouble. It was all the advantage I could get, and it might never come again."

Rita said, "So you forced it on him! And what

did you gain by that?"

"Why," Saxon said, surprised, "I took his measure, girl. He's whang leather all the way through, and he'll chew cactus and spit out the spikes. But he's got a soft spot. Don't you see? He could have killed me, but he was content to shoot the gun out of my hand and let it go at that. He opened himself up like a book and let me read him."

Rita shook her head. They were now beyond the business establishments and nearing a cottage surrounded by a white picket fence. At its gate, Rita took her hand from her father's arm. She looked across the yard to where lamplight burned in a window, and Saxon saw her face soften with the remembrance of another man's hurt.

"Chris is home," she said. "Back to an empty house. Ask him to come out to dinner sometime soon, Dad. It's these first weeks that he's going to miss Sue most." Her lips quirked. "And tell him you've just been the biggest damned fool on Sleeping Cat range."

She opened the gate for him, and he asked, "Where are you going?"

Her smile was bitter. "To Rube's barbershop to borrow a pair of shears. All your way got you was a bloody hand. I'm going to play Delilah to this Texas Samson. Could you use another rider if I hired one?"

Chapter Three: NOBODY'S MAN

KITTREDGE CAME INTO THE HOTEL and crossed its lobby to the desk, men making room for him and the talk of men falling to a faint buzz. He was at once alert to each movement around him, expecting hostility. Every man had his friends, and that fellow who'd just braced him had looked like a person of importance. It was not to Kittredge's liking to have been spotlighted by that incident on the street; he felt edgy and was weary of people and the ways of people. There were times when he envied the small, obscure ones who did the small, obscure tasks of the world. This was one of those times.

The desk clerk, a pimpled youth, said, "Mr. Kittredge? We have a room ready for you," and showed an adolescent awe that would have amused Kittredge another night. You either found the youngsters wide-eyed or else they were the chip-on-the-shoulder kind, wanting to talk hard to a man of his reputation.

"My war sack is over at the stage depot," Kittredge said and put his signature down, adding Texas for an address. He pocketed the extended key and climbed a carpeted stairs to the hall above. From the head of the stairs he took one last look back into the lobby, marking every man's position in a single sweeping glance. Satisfied, he moved on. His room faced on the street and was a good one as cowtown accommodations went. This was not the opulent Cheyenne Club he'd known on his passage north, but it was probably the best Sleeping Cat had to offer.

The door closed behind him; he looked at the bed and the bureau, then moved to the window and looked down upon Sleeping Cat. Presently there came a knock. Kittredge was again wary, but it was only the pimpled clerk fetching his war sack. The clerk came pussyfooting into the room, looking as though he'd like to ask questions. Kittredge had already heard the questions in a dozen towns. He made his face grim and said in a harsh voice, "You reckon this shebang could serve up a catamount steak for supper?" The clerk tried to grin, but he looked scared and made haste to depart.

Afterward Kittredge probed into his fixings and got out his razor and brush and a clean shirt and stripped to the waist and gave himself a washing. He looked in the distorted mirror and saw that he had not forgotten how to smile. Then he shaved. He was wiping the last of the lather away when Gault Telford stepped into the room.

Kittredge came about quickly, crouching like a cat and moving sideward to where he'd hung his gun belt on a bedpost; but Telford said, "Easy, friend. I'm the man you've been expecting. Do you like the room? I reserved the best."

Kittredge said, "Some day you're going to come through a door without knocking, mister, and they'll be dusting out the black wagon for you."

Amusement shone through Telford's thick lenses. Standing, he was a pear-shaped man, scrupulously neat, carefully tailored, a mild and inoffensive man to the eye. Kittredge had seen horses with that same quiet, half-asleep look to them. And he had been pitched into the dust when such horses had exploded beneath him. Here, then, was a deceptively dangerous man, the kind that looked soft from the outside. Kittredge judged him to be about forty, but

Telford had an agelessness that was baffling.

Telford said impatiently, "I think you don't understand. I'm Gault Telford."

"Next time, you knock!"

Telford put his considerable weight down upon a chair and let his satisfaction show. "I like a careful man. As of now, you're working for me."

Strong in Kittredge was the knowledge that which-ever will predominated at his first meeting would hold the whip hand through all of their association; and he said, "As of tomorrow, maybe. Tonight I want a steak an inch thick and a yard wide. And I want to take the stagecoach kinks out of me in that bed. You're a man who jumps to conclusions, mister. And by the way, that letter of yours was damn sketchy."

Telford's serenity remained unruffled. "The re-ports we were getting from Wyoming sounded like all you imported Texas gunmen were in trouble. I didn't know who might get the letter. How did you manage to get out?"

Kittredge shrugged. "We Texas boys got sewed up at the T-A ranch on Crazy Woman Creek with about four hundred of those Wyoming ranchers making it hot for us. I reckon you heard about that. The governor got the army into action, and Colonel Van Horn and his cavalry came along waving a flag of truce. We were all supposed to surrender and be taken to Fort McKinney. That didn't sound good to me, so I slipped away to Buffalo. That's where I got your letter. I hung around Buffalo with my hat pulled low and my lip buttoned tight until the hootin' and hollerin' died down. Then I climbed on the stage."

Telford said, "That was playing it smart. Guns come cheap, but a man doesn't always get brains along with them." He threw out an arm and made a vast circling motion. "This is my town and my range. Sometimes small dogs nip at my heels. Your job will be to kick them out of the way. Two hundred a month and cartridges. Did Wyoming pay you that well?"

Kittredge grinned, but his face stayed sour. "Then you owe me the first cartridge. I used it out on the street. Another thing your letter didn't say was that there'd be a reception committee."

Telford shook his head. "That was Dan Saxon of Circle-S, the only independent rancher left in the basin. If you'd finished him then and there, I'd be shelling out a bonus right now."

"Would you?" Kittredge asked. "That wasn't in the letter, either."

Telford leaned forward, his face like some graven idol's in the semigloom. "Look, friend, you're proddy. Saxon did the unexpected, and that made a surprise for me and a bad moment for you. You got started on the wrong foot tonight, so you're showing me your teeth. I'm not here to play a game with words. There is one chunk of ground in this basin that is not yet mine—Saxon's Circle-S. I've got him nearly to the wall. Money is the sinews of war, and I've just about broke him. I've brought you in to finish the job. Do you want the work?"

"I don't operate from cutbanks in the dark of the

moon."

"You won't have to. Saxon has got one last chance. He knows it and I know it. The railroad is building a spur into the hills. The grading camps need beef, and Saxon has been angling for a contract to supply it. They will pay premium prices, and that cash could be the saving of Circle-S. Therefore I do not want his beef delivered to the railroad. It is as simple as that."

Kittredge said, "It might be interesting." He stood silent then, and thoughtful, a practical man weighing the odds in his mind. But he was also a fanciful man, liking in this proposition the challenge to his imagination and ingenuity. He stood in the gathering dusk, his naked torso gleaming whitely in odd contrast to his sunburned face. He said again, "It might be interesting."

"Then we'll call it a deal," Telford said emphatically and arose.

"Not yet," Kittredge said.

Telford frowned. "Why not?"

"You're a man who takes things for granted—including doors. You need a lesson in politeness, mister, and one in patience. Come around tomorrow morning and we'll talk again."

All the affability went out of Telford, but the metallic rage that rose in his eyes didn't quite explode from his lips. He stood for a moment making an inward fight that showed plain on him; and then he said, "To a man like you, I would give free rein on any job. I would ask no questions as long as the job was done. But I demand respect. Do you understand that?"

Kittredge grinned again. "The thing you're forgetting is that I'm not working for you yet. Come around tomorrow."

Telford's shoulders bunched angrily, but he crossed the room and put his hand to the doorknob. He had a surprisingly light walk for a man so heavy. He said, "I choose to think that your long trip has tired you and that what happened between you and Saxon was a further drain on your nerves. Because I choose to think that, I shall overlook your attitude."

Kittredge's grin broadened. "Good. That's as close to a deal as we need come right now. You choose to think what you damn well please, and I'll choose to think my way. Good night, Mr. Telford."

After Telford had closed the door, Kittredge was of a mind to turn the key; but he didn't. He went again to the window and stared down upon Sleeping Cat. In him was a slow anger and an old rebellion. You put yourself up for hire; and the Gault Telfords sent for you, wanting not only your gun skill but every part of you, inside and out. You had your price; and when that was planked down on the barrelhead, your self-respect was supposed to be tossed into the bargain. That was the way of it. He had met the Gault Telfords before, and the only difference in a pattern grown dull with repetition was one town and another. And even the towns got so they looked the same.

With such thinking his weariness became more than physical. And so he stood and watched the night enfold Sleeping Cat while the lamps blossomed to yellow the dusty street. He got the makings from his discarded shirt and fashioned a cigarette, being careful that the match light didn't show. This was a habitual wariness. He heard the distant tinkling of a saloon piano and above it the high-pitched laughter of a percentage girl. This turned his mind to Cora Dufrayne, who had gone her way once the stage reached Sleeping Cat. The remembrance of her stirred him, and he wondered where she'd gone.

He let his eyes rove the street again and saw the red eye of a forge in the open doorway of a shop where a blacksmith worked late. Metal clanged against metal, making a steady rhythm that rose in the night and carried his thinking backward. He remembered another town and another night and a blacksmith who'd worked late, and when he strove for total recall, it came to him that his horse had thrown a shoe and the minutes had counted then, for there'd been muttering on the street and men gathering against him. But he could not remember the name of the town. All of his memories had become like this, vague and shadow-edged, with a taint of nightmare to them; and all the towns were a blend in his mind and something better forgotten.

At the tap on the door, he swung about, fretful and frowning. He supposed that Telford had returned, and he was in no mood for Telford. He said, "Come in."

A girl opened the door and stood framed against the hall's lamplight, and he at once remembered her as the one who'd come rushing to the man he'd shot, that Dan Saxon. He still hadn't donned his shirt, and he was suddenly conscious of this and made a move toward the fresh one he'd laid out on the bed.

The girl said, "I'm Rita Saxon."

He gave her a level look. "And you've come to tell me what you think of that business on the street." This, too, was part of an ancient pattern; sometimes it was a hysterical widow, babbling recriminations, sometimes a frosty-eyed brother or father with a gun in his fist.

"No," she said, "I've come to say there are no hard feelings. Aren't you going to ask me in?"

He picked up the shirt and got into it and buttoned it after a fashion. He made a poor job of tucking the shirt into his pants. He lifted his gun belt from the bedpost and swung it around his middle and got it latched, then moved to the bureau and got the lamp lighted. Looking at Rita, he shrugged. "Come in, if you wish. What's on your mind?"

In the lamplight she was a mighty pretty girl with that soft olive skin and those eyes that took a man back to Texas and languid Rio nights. She moved gracefully, and he liked that. She came into the room and closed the door and put her back to it. She smiled at him, her smile warm and inviting. His thought was that he'd twice been stirred by women today, but he was warier of this one.

"I've been waiting," she said. "I knew you had company, but I saw him come downstairs. Is it too late to ask you to change sides?"

Kittredge asked, "You're fetching me an offer from Circle-S?"

"Forty a month and found," she said. "Moving a bunch of cattle up into the hills. Long hours and hard ones. Cold blankets and early risings and no pay till the job is done. It doesn't begin to meet Telford's offer, does it?"

He grimaced. "Not yet!"

She came farther into the room; she affected a liquid way of walking, a sinuous movement to her hips. She smiled at him again, and this time her smile was an invitation and a challenge. She said, "I'm sure you'll find it pleasant working for Circle-S. I'll try to make it so."

Now he understood, and he threw back his head and laughed. His laughter boomed in the room and filled the corners, making a great, rolling sound. He saw her smile fade and chagrin draw down her lips, and she said, "Whatever is funny must only be funny to you."

He said, "I've seen hussies try to play the part of ladies. That was bad enough. But not nearly so funny as a lady trying to play a hussy."

She took a step nearer and said with quick anger that made her eyes stormy, "You needn't draw any inference! What I said implied no promise."

"Of course not," he said and laughed again. "That's where the joke comes in. I'm to go to work for Circle-S. At the end of a day's work, if I'm not so dead beat out that I can't think of anything but hitting my soogans, the boss's beautiful daughter will maybe go riding with me. When I try to kiss her, she'll tuck in her chin, but she'll do it with a laugh so I'll be fool enough to try another night. Between times, she'll shake her hips at me and say all the things a man can take two ways. We'll play that kind of cheating game till the work's done. Then I'll get my forty a month. And the boss's daughter will be mighty busy whenever I come around."

Color crept into her face, and he was sure she was going to slap him. Instead, she said, "You demand payment in advance, is that it?"

Her boldness caught him off balance. She was all femininity in the lamplight, desirable and wholly within reach; yet there was about her a forthrightness that puzzled him. He said soberly, "You're bluffing."

She turned back toward the door. He thought she was going to slam through it angrily, but she twisted the key and then faced about. She said in a small voice, "Circle-S has little enough left to offer. Probably Telford told you that. I see you want your bargains pat. You can come right out and name it now."

That was when he saw that she was scared—scared, yet brave and determined. He stared at her, not believing what she implied, yet having to believe it; for there was the locked door. In that moment all the laughter went out of him, and he hated Gault Telford and himself and all his way of life. She stood there for the taking, and his blood thundered in his temples, but it was her willingness that defeated him. For he could tell from what desperation her willingness was wrought.

He said in a softer voice, "Understand this. I was born twenty years too late. Once a man could swing a wide loop in the Texas brush and build up a herd from the mavericks that belonged to ranchers scattered to hellangone by the war. Anybody could become a cattle king overnight, and a lot of them did. Maybe your dad was one of those. But I had to come along too late. For me and my kind it's supposed to be forty bucks a month. But when I was old enough to think, I decided I'd play for bigger stakes, or I wouldn't play at all. That's what fetched me from Texas to Wyoming. That's what fetched me here. Gault Telford offered the biggest stake. That's all there is to it."

Rita said, "And where'll your trail take you? From one gun job to another! Until some day *you're* the old man who stands in the street and faces a young man the way my father faced you today."

He shook his head. "I'll have a ranch of my own before that day. I'm no fool who earns it fast and spends it fast. This town, this job, is just one rock in the crossing of a wide creek."

She had dropped all pretense of coquetry; her fire now was genuine. "That's nothing but plain selfishness! I ought to feel sorry for you!"

"What's the difference between us?" he demanded. "What I want, I go after in my own way. You have your way. It just happens that I don't want to buy your bargain."

She said, "Here's the difference—what *I'd* be willing to do is for somebody else—an old man who spent his last chip tonight."

"Sure," he said. "And that's why it would be only half a bargain."

Her chin came up. "The Saxons gamble, but they never cheat!"

"I wonder," he said. He walked toward her, and she stood, not flinching. He hooked his hands under her arms and lifted her from her feet. Swinging her up, he got an arm under her knees and held her thus cradled and saw the fear naked in her eyes, and the courage. He crossed to the bed and tossed her there and turned and fumbled at the key in the door, unlocking it. He went out into the hall, leaving the door half-open behind him, and started for the stairs.

Halfway down the stairs, he said, "Hell!" softly. Then he began laughing again and came into the lobby laughing. It struck him that the sour taste Gault Telford had left in his mouth had been washed away.

Chapter Four: LAMPLIGHT AND DARKNESS

IN THE HOUSE of Dr. Christopher Farrell, Dan Saxon, aware of the accumulated mustiness of two weeks of locked doors and closed windows, welcomed the heady smell of disinfectant as Farrell worked on his wounded hand. When pain came, Saxon fixed his eyes on the ceiling and put his teeth together. The bandage in place, he wriggled his fingers which had been left exposed, and said, "That's a good piece of work, Chris," and relaxed in the green plush chair. Wry humor made crow's-feet at the corners of his eyes. "Just reach into my coat and get your pay from my wallet. Maybe the word hasn't got to you yet, but I'm on a cash basis."

Farrell straightened himself and unrolled his sleeves. "You'll be a bit clumsy," he said, his voice crisply professional, "but you should have no trouble. Rita can change the bandage, and I'll drop around later for a look."

"Do that," Saxon said and made no move to go. They were in Farrell's parlor, and Saxon liked the room with its lace curtains and red drapes held by white cords with tassels. The most peaceful room in Sleeping Cat Basin, he told himself, a bit of the Midwest moved to Montana's raw plains. It had a Franklin stove and a music box and a cut-glass trimmed ceiling lamp. It had all the signs of Sue Farrell's gentleness and good taste, and her ghost walked here. Saxon could see that in Farrell's sensitive face. A white, drawn face. Queer, Saxon thought, no matter how many basin roads Farrell traveled, the sun never seemed to touch him.

Saxon asked gently, "How was it at Miles City?"

"A beautiful funeral," Farrell said. "Sue's folks saw to that. I'm glad I took her body there. It made it easier for them."

Saxon asked, "And now?"

Farrell shrugged and took a chair across from Saxon. He sat staring, his fingers turning the wedding ring on his left hand until Saxon had the feeling of being entirely alone in the room. Saxon said then, gruffly, "Look, Chris, neither you nor anybody else could have cured her."

"I know that," Farrell said. "I suppose it's one of the compensations of being a doctor. I'll never have to wonder if something couldn't have been done. Heart trouble was in her family. Her older sister went the same way."

Saxon stirred uneasily, seeing before him a troubled man who owned his friendship, wanting to help that man. After a brief while Saxon asked, "How long have you been here, Chris? Two years—three?"

"Two. I came in the spring of '90."

Saxon's eyes moved about this room where Sue Farrell had dwelt. "Time to be moving on," he said. "A young man should look over a lot of landscape before he puts down roots. It gives him memories when the rheumatism gets him."

Farrell smiled a bitter smile in the lamplight. "Nebraska, maybe, or some other safe, settled country. You think I could run away from it, eh, Dan?"

Saxon showed genuine surprise. "Run from what, Chris?"

"You knew about the Jimsons."

"Those bully boys who used to ride for the Rocking-T? They're still grub-lining around the range, I'm told. Yes, I heard you had some kind of brush with them. What's that got to do with what we're talking about?"

"It was about eight weeks ago," Farrell said, his voice gone dull. "They were in town and drinking, and I met them out on the street. I suppose I've always looked like a tenderfoot to them. They made me dance, Dan. They peppered bullets about my feet and made me perform like a crazy fool. I was waiting for Sue, who'd gone into Barney Shay's. She stood there on the mercantile's porch and saw the whole thing. So help me, Dan, that's one reason why I took the insult. My main thought was what might happen if I showed fight and those drunken savages started shooting every direction."

Saxon's eyes squinted reflectively. "So that's been bothering you!"

Pain showed in Farrell's eyes, but he kept his face blank. "Sue was a Westerner, Dan. In spite of her gentleness and her quiet ways, she was a Westerner through and through. Her folks brought cattle up from Texas in the seventies, and it's only in recent years that they've lived in town."

Saxon nodded. "I knew the family."

"I practiced for a year in Miles," Farrell went on. "That's where I met Sue. I used to wonder why she married me; I think now she must have felt some attraction of opposites. Or maybe she wanted someone to mother. But the truth must have grown pretty obvious. If the need existed, I could take off your leg with a jackknife and hand it to you, but just the same, I'm a physical coward. Sue knew it. She knew I didn't fit in this country. The Jimson episode only proved it. Her last words to me were, 'Take care of yourself, Chris.'"

"Hell, those were about the last words my wife said to me," Saxon observed. "The only difference was that she said them in Spanish."

"She didn't mean the same thing," Farrell insisted. "I know you, Dan. You're the only real friend I've made in this basin. That's why I'm talking like this. I'm sure you've never known what it's like to be afraid of your own shadow."

Saxon smiled wryly. "You should have been in my skin about half an hour ago!"

"I met the Jimsons again today," Farrell continued, his face showing the agony of that memory. "They stopped the stagecoach a few miles south of here. There were two other passengers aboard, a woman named Cora Dufrayne, with whom I'd ridden from Miles, and a man calling himself Kittredge who came up from the south. All the Jimsons wanted was a little poker money, I guess; they must have known the stage carries no treasure box. They lined us up and ordered us to turn out our pockets. Kittredge had gone to get a drink. He came back and got behind the Jimsons. They'd just decided the Dufrayne woman was hiding jewelry, and they proposed to tear the clothes off her. I went a little crazy then. Perhaps it's because now I see something of Sue in every woman. Kittredge sent a shot close enough to stop me, then got the drop on the Jimsons. He wanted their guns lifted. The Dufrayne woman did that for him."

Saxon's long face puckered with thought. "I suppose the real reason you wanted to jump the Jimsons was that you've been fretting over what happened on the street. Since you've never packed a gun, that was a damned foolish notion, Chris."

Farrell said, "You miss the point. The woman stepped forward to take the guns away from the Jimsons. She'd sensed how inept I was. Fear must have been standing out on me."

Saxon said slowly, "Or maybe she wanted to impress Kittredge. I can see how a woman might want to do that."

"You know him?"

Saxon smiled his wry smile again and held up his bandaged hand. "He gave me this."

Farrell shook his head. "I never ask a patient a question, even when he's my friend. That's one lesson Montana has so far taught me."

"This will be no secret," Saxon said. "With Sue in her last illness and then dying, you lost touch. That makes you the only man in Sleeping Cat who hasn't known for a month that Gault Telford was sending for Kittredge. He's a hired gunman brought in to finish me."

"Then that gives me a reason to hate him," Farrell said, his face darkening. "He's a savage, Dan, minus the feathers and the scalp lock. He's of the cut of the Jimsons, except that he has more intelligence. Which makes him only the more dangerous."

"No," Saxon said. "He's just a cowhand who took a wrong turn of the trail somewhere. Think kindly of him. You might even do well to feel sorry for him. Some day he will come face to face with himself, and that will not be a happy day for him."

"I'm afraid I'm not equipped with your kind of tolerance, Dan."

Saxon got out of the chair and reached for his long coat and managed to get into it in spite of his bandaged hand. He picked his sombrero from a chair and set it at a rakish angle and turned toward the door. "Rita wants you to drop out for dinner some Sunday," he said, wondering what else to say. Christopher Farrell had laid himself bare tonight, and the

sight of him thus exposed had stunned Dan Saxon
and sickened him a little. He wanted now the words
that might help Farrell fight his own fear, but courage was not something you dug out of your pocket
like a spare four bits and handed to a friend. He
thought again of Kittredge and remembered how
Farrell's eyes had looked when he, Saxon, had spoken
of Kittredge, and he saw one truth.

He said, "I think, Chris, that you resent Kittredge
because he represents what you choose to call physical courage. In other words, you see him as your
opposite and, in a sense, the man you'd like to be.
But there's one question you'd better ask yourself.
Everything considered, would you want to change
skins with him?"

Farrell said, "I shall always hate the breed of man
who rides roughshod over the earth. Kittredge is that
kind." His voice turned professional again, closing
out Saxon. "Take care of that hand."

"Sure," Saxon said and went out into the night.

Kittredge took his solitary meal in the hotel dining-room. At this late hour there was little supper
trade, and he was glad to be apart from others. He
was a man whose thoughts always turned inward, for
his profession kept him on a lonely path, and he
had thus learned communion with the night winds
and the far reaches, sharing these things with no
man but the inner one. There was that star upon
which his eye was fixed, the one he'd spoken of to
Rita Saxon; and he'd adopted one truism and kept
carefully to it—the man traveled the fastest who

traveled alone. Yet tonight he was acutely conscious when gay laughter lifted from a crowded table where a family took its meal; and he marked the comings and goings of pairs of people, wondering about them, wondering about their camaraderie.

Once he'd known the feeling of belonging, in the bunkhouses of far Texas, when he'd been a working cowhand who had come to resent his station. After that, he'd examined his skills and found only one that set him a notch above other men. His first gun job had been a little brawl along the Brazos, but there'd been a hefty bonus when the smoke cleared away, and he'd salted it down, every cent of it.

There had been other such jobs since. Then those men from the big cattle interests in Wyoming had come recruiting for that Johnson County trouble, and he'd been aboard that special train that left Denver over the Union Pacific for northern Wyoming. He had to smile, remembering that they'd even had two war correspondents along, that fellow from the Chicago *Herald* and the one from the Cheyenne *Sun*. And Reb Kittredge had really made a name for himself at the siege on Crazy Woman Creek, even though the Wyoming invasion had turned into a debacle.

He'd got that letter from Gault Telford and come farther north to sell his skill once more. But there was a perverseness in him that had made him hate his employers in Texas and Wyoming and take a sudden dislike to Telford. It was always the big ones who hired guns. Still, their money was good; it made a solid feel in the pocket and a pretty scrawl in a bank book. But that girl in his room tonight had shaken his convictions about both money and people; and so, eating alone now, he wondered about those from whom he'd set himself apart, ordinary, unimportant people who laughed at their suppers.

He had known something of this feeling before; he had found himself at strange bars and seen in a laughing cowpoke a resemblance to somebody he'd ridden with in Texas. Maybe it was the voice or a mannerism. Once in a while he'd bought a drink and made small talk, but there was always an emptiness; he had found no bridge to the lost yesterdays.

His meal finished tonight, he came again to the lobby and saw Rita there. She sat in one of the chairs, alongside her father, whose right hand was now wrapped in a serviceable bandage. Kittredge nudged the brim of his Stetson and gave Rita a smile. Rita's glance was straight, but she didn't smile back. Dan Saxon nodded, showing no malice; and Kittredge wondered how much of what had transpired upstairs Rita had told her father.

Kittredge asked, "How's your hand?"

"A bad scratch," Saxon said.

Kittredge stood studying him, seeing in Saxon both intelligence and courage; and the memory of that shooting before the stage station was real only because of the bandaged hand. Kittredge's face hardened. "And when you're healed enough so you can handle a gun again?"

Saxon smiled. "Remember what I said on the street? I know an ace when I see one face up. I haven't got the cards to buck it."

Kittredge's face unfroze, and he smiled again at Rita. "Are you as wise as your father?"

The heat of anger showed in Rita's eyes. "Some day, somewhere, you'll meet a man who'll bring you to your knees. I hope I'm there when that day comes!"

Kittredge said gravely, "Perhaps," no irony in him.

He touched his hatbrim again and went out into the street. Around him, Sleeping Cat's night life swirled; he could hear the clatter of the saloons and the constant rumble of men's voices; and as he moved along the street, he had to elbow his way against a steady, pressing tide. He saw that the blacksmith shop he'd spied from his hotel window was now closed. He tried again to remember that other town where a forge had blazed in the night, but the name still eluded him. He thought, *The hell with it!*

He wanted the special feel of Sleeping Cat, the thorough knowledge that might stand him in good stead before his work here was finished. He saw horses crowding all the hitchracks and memorized their brands without conscious intention; he saw the number of bearded, booted railroad workers and studied them as one breed of man studies another. A week's pay in their pants, and the lid lifted! They were like the cowhands and the trail drifters and the frock-coated gamblers, living one day at a time and asking only of life a bottle and a deck of cards and a painted woman. Considering this, some of his surety returned and with it a studied arrogance, for he was a man with an eye on tomorrow.

He passed a print shop and a millinery and a saddle shop, all dark at this hour. A single lantern glowed deep within the recesses of a livery stable; beyond this was Sleeping Cat's only brick building— the bank. He looked at the gold lettering on the bank's window, but Gault Telford's name wasn't there. Kittredge hadn't expected it would be. The Telfords always held to the center of the web, dark and quiet as spiders. He remembered what Telford had said about this being his town.

Down here, on the fringe of the business establishments, he came upon a hitchrail in the shadow of a giant cottonwood and saw three tied horses. He looked at them, and memory stirred, and he came closer, peering hard. He knew them then, and with the knowledge his wariness turned sharp. Those horses called up to him a picture of the bearded Jimson brothers tied backward in their saddles, the three of them crazy with humiliation and anger. He made an estimate of elapsed time and judged that they must have soon freed themselves of the ropes. In the darkness he grinned at the spectacle they'd made, then walked on.

When he'd got as far as Doc Farrell's cottage, he crossed over and walked back along the far side of the street. He moved slowly, wary always of the shadowy slots between buildings, wary of any man who looked at him twice. This was instinctive, this being constantly ready. Sometimes he grew weary of it. But tonight there were the Jimsons. He no longer grinned at thought of them; they would be nursing a hate that had made them bold enough to show in

town on the heels of their attempted holdup. He
was a man who fought for pay, not for pleasure;
and he wanted none of the Jimsons.

Suddenly he thought of his bed in the hotel, and
the weariness of long traveling came upon him. But
now he was beyond the hotel and nearing the Bagdad, and he promised himself one drink, and turned
in through the swinging doors. He was mildly astonished at the size of the place and its opulence;
he had expected nothing like this in Sleeping Cat.
The bar was long, and there were at least a score
of gaming-tables. A small stage filled one end of the
room. Smoke lay in blue layers, and a piano tinkled
incessantly; and a hundred men were here, cowboys
and construction workers and citizens of the town.
He elbowed among these and got to the bar and
ordered whisky and took his time with it, his eyes
always on the bar mirror so that he could see who-
ever approached his back.

There was an upstairs to this place, he observed,
with a balcony running around three sides of the
main barroom. He caught a glimpse of the gay skirt
of a percentage girl on the runway above and understood. Here was a place providing all the pleasures.
The whisky warmed him and took some of the
tension out of him and gave him a sense of well-
being. He listened to the rumble of talk all around
him. He thought again of bed and was of a mind
to turn away. But the bartender worked toward him
and asked, "Reb Kittredge?"

Kittredge nodded.

The bartender laid down silver and said, "I didn't

know you when I took your money. This is Gault Telford's place, so you drink on the house. He left orders."

"Put it in your pocket," Kittredge said. "I don't start work till the morning shift."

The bartender inclined his head. "Walk upstairs," he said. "First door to the right."

Kittredge's lips turned tight. "I've already had my talk with him. I'll see him tomorrow."

"It wasn't him sent me word who you are," the bartender said. "Was I you, I'd go upstairs."

Kittredge shrugged and moved away, a certain rebellion rising in him. He saw to one side of the little stage the stairs that led upward. He had a long moment's reflection, and a strong feeling that to climb those stairs would commit him in a way he would come to regret. Shrugging, he ascended and turned toward the right. The door was open for him, and Cora Dufrayne stood there. Instinct still whispered that this rendezvous was not for him, but he stepped inside; and when he had done so, she closed the door behind him.

Chapter Five: DEATH WAITS

LAMPLIGHT WAS KIND TO CORA, giving her face a softness that made her much younger, but her eyes were bold and showed both an invitation and a grave concern. Kittredge had expected to find her in the short, spangled skirt of a percentage girl; she wore, instead, a long russet gown of good material that clung tightly to her, enhancing the roundness of her figure, making her even more statuesque than he'd remembered her at the stage station. The gown was cut to leave her shoulders and forearms bare; her breasts showed a shadowy cleft. Her yellow, high-piled hair was held by an ornate comb; her earrings were of elegant jade. Her perfume reached to Kittredge and was heady in his nostrils, and he was deeply stirred in spite of himself.

To cover any show of confusion, he laughed and said, "Telford lied. He claimed he'd reserved the best room in town for *me*."

He'd deliberately taken his eyes from her and was looking about the room. Here were draped windows and a bed with a ruffled spread. The rug was soft under his feet, and the lamp on the teakwood table was of hand-painted china. He was puzzled both by the room and the gown she wore, not quite understanding her position in this place, but he could draw only one inference. He laughed again, and seeing Cora frown, he said, "It just strikes me as funny that we both came here to work for him. Each in our own way."

She said with a certain dignity, "You saw the stage downstairs. I sing here. No more than that, unless I choose."

He decided then that she was straightforward rather than bold, and he felt a sudden kinship to her and knew that it had been there from the first, unrealized, drawing them together. He sensed that her trail had been as rocky as his, her schooling his own harsh kind. They were of a lost breed, drifting in loneliness toward some far star, finding no man close to them, and no woman. He remembered her travel-scarred trunk that had told him so much; it stood in yonder corner, out of place in such opulent surroundings. He became a gentler man with a gentler voice. "I didn't ask."

She said swiftly, "I saw you from the balcony. I signaled the bartender and got word to you. Reb, those three brothers are in town. They came to the bar less than half an hour ago."

"I saw their horses," he said.

She sighed. "I was afraid for you. They are the kind who would play it safe. A bullet from behind."

He lifted his shoulders and let them fall, a cool man making his acceptance. "Some day, somewhere, I suppose. Them or someone like them. That chance goes with being in my business. I've grown used to being careful."

A silence came between them, and in that silence the bedlam of the saloon seeped around the door and was like a distant rumor traveling in the night, the muted murmur of many voices, the tinkling of glasses, the steady, tuneless beat of the piano.

Cora made a movement with her hand and said, "Won't you sit down? I have wine, if you favor it."

The chairs were plush-padded and handsomely carved. He turned one around and straddled it, folding his arms on its back. This was a pretty fancy seat for a man used to saddle leather. He grinned. "I favor whisky, but I've had all I promised myself tonight."

She moved with a swish of skirts and put herself before him though at a distance, and he wondered if this was a calculated pose. She stood with her face half shadowed; she was, he decided, far more attractive than he'd realized. Her hands were eloquent; her movements were sensuous, eternally feminine; but he had hold of himself now. It had become a game of waiting; they were done with her excuse for calling him here; and whatever her real reason, it would come out. He supposed there would be a certain amount of parrying, but he had overlooked her straightforwardness.

She said, "I told you I only sing here. Yet I have been no better than any other girl in this place. Somewhere along the way, I learned a lesson. What men most desire is the unattainable. Gault Telford is the kind who understands that. You think that perhaps I'm his kept woman. Then you don't know Telford. No woman or man represents any more to him than cash in the till. He knows I'll bring trade here because the men who come once will come again—hoping. And I shall sing for them again and again; that is all I have bargained to do."

He said bluntly, "But there'll be a last song, a day when you're old and unattractive."

"Yes," she said. "Such a day will come."

"And then?"

"I shall have prepared myself for that day. I shall own a place like this before then."

He said, "So?" but he had grown very attentive.

Her face turned harsh. "I'm from Texas, too, Reb. Had you guessed that? I've known every dirty honky-tonk between San Antonio and Miles City. I've starved and frozen, and I've known nights when I've hated the sight of a man. I've learned that you get only what you take from life. I've looked for such a place as this, and now I've found it. This is my last stop. To me, Gault Telford is a fat turkey to be plucked. What he's got by grabbing can be grabbed away from him. I've told no one about this but you."

"Because you saw that *I* was after something besides a day's eating and sleeping?"

She shrugged. "Never ask a woman how she knows such things."

He took a match from his pocket and snapped it between his fingers. "That for Telford, eh?"

"Reb," she said very intently, "have you ever thought why there are some like Telford who own places like this and ranches and cattle and some like us who only draw their pay?"

"Ah, yes," he said and smiled.

"But you are not satisfied it should be that way?"

He spread his hands and looked at them. He said, "I go to work for him tomorrow morning. To me he is only a stepping-stone, one more job along the way. Some day there will be a last job. But while I work for Telford, he'll never have to fear turning his back to me. A man must have some point of pride, and that's mine. But what you've told me tonight will not go beyond this room. Be sure of that."

She said, "A man can afford to have that pride. My only weapon is ruthlessness. It's a man's world, Reb. What part in yours will a woman play?"

"I haven't let myself think about that," he said. "When I've lifted my heel off the last stepping-stone, it may be different. Then, maybe, I'll want a woman to share what I've got."

"But until that day you'll be wary?"

"Damn wary," he said.

"Too wary to make a bargain with a woman?"

He looked at her and saw no guile in her face. He asked, "What kind of bargain?"

"Together we could make this our last stop. Together we could topple over Gault Telford. No woman could do that job alone. I need you behind me, Reb."

"Why me?"

"Because we talk the same language. And if we run into rough work before the job is done, you'll be able to handle that end of it."

He said, "And that's all you'd want of me?"

"No more than that," she said.

He rose then, an acute sense of disappointment in him. He moved to the door and took a stand there and said, "You might have been the woman I'd want when the time came to sit in the sun. But you wouldn't do. I'll tell you why, Cora. It's because I'm no more to you than the gun I pack at my hip. You see, I've grown tired, too. Tired of being nothing but a gun in the minds of men and women alike. I don't think we could hang a partnership on that kind of peg."

He put his hand to the door, but she moved swiftly, crying, "Wait, Reb!"

She came to him with a certain fierceness and pressed herself against him, putting her arms around his neck. In the warmth of this room, the warmth of her body became his and was wholly desirable; he felt the firmness of her and the softness and had a mad moment when he was almost swept beyond thinking. She had made him two offers, and her mistake was that she had not made this one first. There would be no completion in her caresses, no full giving, and knowing this, he disengaged her arms.

He looked at her and was now remote from her, seeing her as a hard woman and an unhappy one. He said, "Good luck to you, Cora. I shall keep wishing you that."

He supposed she would be angry, but she stood back from him and showed an inward smiling that held its own sadness. "I think you will always ride alone, Reb."

He shrugged. "Maybe."

She made a gesture with her hand. "I'm scheduled to sing in a very few minutes. Stay and hear me."

He showed a wintry smile. "So that I shall come back again and again?"

"No," she said. "I want you to hear me because singing, at least, is a thing I do well."

"I'll stay," he promised.

He went out to the head of the stairs, and all the saloon sounds rose and engulfed him and put an edge to his nerves. He descended into this bedlam and thought of whisky, feeling the need for a drink; but he had disciplined himself against such appetites, and he began working his way through the press of humanity to a place near the door. A percentage girl plucked at his sleeve, but he shook his head. He passed a blackjack table and gave it a glance with no real interest; all his life was a gamble, so he had no need for the artificial kind. He got to the far wall and put his back to it and waited.

Remembering Cora, he was a disappointed man, with a still, slow-burning anger in him. He thought of those last moments in her room, and he thought, too, of Rita Saxon, who had also flung herself at him; and he laughed then, thinking, *Twice in one night!*

He felt eyes on him and became aware of a man's close scrutiny, and this reminded him of the Jimsons, but the one who stared was a weather-burned, youngish man. Kittredge recalled the fellow; this was the one who had come with Rita Saxon to her wounded father. He didn't like the steady appraisal of the man; it held a certain belligerency, and he asked gruffly, "What's on your mind?"

Curly Mather said, "That depends."

"You work for Saxon?"

"Foreman. I'm supposed to be on my way back to the ranch. I'm staying here instead. Until Dan's ready to leave."

"To keep an eye on me?"

"Dan's a damn fool. He might try twice."

"Run along," Kittredge said and was suddenly a disgusted man. "Take your face somewhere else!"

Mather said, hard-voiced, "I go where I please," but he moved away and became lost in the crowd.

The curtain on the little stage jerked open. The man at the piano beat out a fanfare of sorts, and Kittredge saw Cora on the low platform. She had not changed her gown; she came forward to the sputtering kerosene footlights and gave the crowd a smile and a curtsy and stepped back. Her hands clasped before her, she began singing in a low, throaty voice.

"The years creep slowly by, Lorena;
The dew is on the grass again,
The sun's low down the sky, Lorena;
The frost gleams where the flowers have been."

The house had hushed down. She had chained all
these men by her voice, but it was more than that
that held them; she had touched the romanticism in
them, and the loneliness; she had made of herself the
embodiment of all the girls left behind and all the
girls unattainable. She was sin and sweetness, pain
and pleasure. Her eyes found Kittredge in the crowd,
and he had the feeling that she sang only to him.

"A hundred months have passed, Lorena,
Since last I held your hand in mine
And felt your pulse beat fast, Lorena,
Though mine beat faster far than thine."

Her singing went on, changing in words, changing
in spirit until sometimes it was a wild tumult, sometimes a sad whispering. Then she made her curtsy
again, and the curtains closed. The applause racketed
upward, made of hands and boots and hoarse shouting; and he glimpsed Cora climbing the stairs. At the
top she turned and gave him one last glance that held
both a moment's appeal and a faint mockery. Then
she was gone. The voices became a roaring bedlam
again; a spangled-skirted percentage girl appeared on
the stage, kicking high, and the piano went wild.

Kittredge turned to leave and found Gault Telford
beaming at him through his glasses. Telford asked,

"How did you like Cora?"

Kittredge shrugged. "She can sing."

Again Telford looked like a half-asleep horse. "I saw you come downstairs a few minutes ago. You met her on the stagecoach, I suppose."

Kittredge asked harshly, "What of it?"

Telford spread his hands. "You weren't enthusiastic about my offer when we talked earlier. Perhaps something more than money might interest you. If Cora wasn't kind to you, just say the word. I'll have a talk with her."

Kittredge looked at this paunchy man, so scrupulously neat, so splendidly tailored, this man who used any kind of coin, and he said, "Get the hell out of my way," and shoved hard at Telford with his shoulder as he went by him. He might have dumped Telford over except for the press of the crowd. He didn't look back at Telford.

He came out of the Bagdad and started up the street for the hotel. All the proper business places were now darkened and locked, but the boardwalks still teemed. He felt like smashing his fist against something; he felt tired of people and the ways of people. He drew in the air of outdoors and liked it, feeling less tense. He thought, *Tomorrow I go to work for him,* and was tempted to catch the first stage out of here; but he knew his trail would only take him to another Telford. He moved on and came to a part of the street where the crowd had thinned out. He liked the aloneness here and stopped in a patch of darkness between the flung lights of two saloons and rolled up a quirly and put a match to it. He held the match overlong, his mind jaded, his senses dull.

He had this one moment of unwariness, and in it the flat crash of the gun came, to be caught by the false fronts and sent bounding along the street. Lead splintered the weather-warped siding of the building by which he stood, and he thought he'd felt the air-lash of the bullet. He flung the cigarette from him in one swift movement, and at the same time flung himself downward and went rolling.

Chapter Six: CUT OF THE CARDS

HIS ONE WILD THOUGHT WAS, *The Jimsons!* And he cursed himself for his carelessness. Across the street, the gun beat again, the bullet going high to find solid lodging somewhere behind him. Kittredge ceased his rolling and got on his hands and knees and lifted his head, peering. The movement of men made a blur along the far boardwalk; wayfarers scurried frantically, wanting themselves out of gun range. One of these raised a roaring protest.

Kittredge got on one knee and got his gun into his hand, and was at once aware that he made a fine target for night-sharpened eyes. Mindful that many men were across the way, he held his fire, hoping the bushwhacker would shoot again so that he might mark the gun flash. Boots beat hard against the yonder planking, and Kittredge judged that the gunman was taking to cover, not daring to fire again lest he be seen at such work. Kittredge came to his feet and faded backward between the buildings. Deep in the shadows he paused, a cold and calculating man; and in that moment the hunted became the hunter.

His man, he judged, had sought the far alley and would either call it a night or wait his chance to make a second play. But now it had become a game for two, and Kittredge groped carefully behind the buildings until he reached the Bagdad, then came again to the boardwalk he'd quitted. Here the crowd pressed thick and made cover for him. Holding his right arm straight down and keeping his gun unobtrusively close to his body, he boldly crossed over, moved along until he found a passage between two buildings and gained the alley. He began walking very slowly; he tested each step before he took it and was wary of trash barrels and heaped debris. Often he paused and listened, standing still and attentive, his ears cocked for furtive footsteps. In this manner he slowly paralleled the main street.

He had come close enough to death to be angry, but this was a luxury he could not allow himself, not if he was to keep a clear head. He was stalking dangerous game, and he reflected that it might not even be one of the Jimsons.

The seeds of death could lie in a wrong judgment, and he put his mind to all the possibilities. There was Gault Telford, whom he'd so violently shoved in the Bagdad. Telford was not the gun-toting kind, but Telford might have ordered a houseman to cut after Kittredge. Still, Telford wanted a live Kittredge, not a dead one. He remembered that zealous young foreman of Circle-S, who had disobeyed Dan Saxon's orders out of a sort of loyalty. A rash man and a ready one. It was very important to know whom you were up against. Only one man had done the shooting; he was sure of that.

Kittredge's mind went back to the Jimsons. Had the three of them split up, the better to cover the town?

Something stirred in the shadows, and Kittredge instantly crouched, his eyes and ears questing hard. A gaunt dog, sniffing at a trash barrel, went scurrying away, showing briefly in the light from an open back door. Kittredge thought, *I'm getting spooky!* and was sick of this business.

But he was a man with a wildcat by the tail, and so he traversed the length of the alley, taking a good hour at the task. He moved in a world of silence and darkness just a few yards from the street; he moved alone, with the sounds of Sleeping Cat all around him, yet a million miles away. The Bagdad's piano reached him; once he thought he heard Cora's distant voice in an old, old song. He sensed that the town was gradually quieting down; some were riding out of Sleeping Cat, basin cowboys who would have to answer an early call. He could hear the soft plop of hoofs in the street's dust, the whisky-thickened voices of trail partners talking.

He worked his way back to the boardwalk and came carefully to that far cottonwood with the isolated hitchrack where the Jimsons had left their mounts. The rack was empty.

In him then was a strong conviction that it had indeed been a Jimson who'd made the try. This indicated departure of the brothers fitted the pattern of their kind. Dull brains worked in dull ways. Anger would have fetched them rampaging into town, in spite of the danger of arrest. Brute pride would have sent them gunning in the night. Fear would have driven them out when their attempt had failed.

He cased his gun then and beat the dust from his clothes, letting himself have his moment of anger as he remembered rolling in the street. This was a closed page, but the next would be turned when again his trail crossed with that of the bearded brothers. He thought of the bed in the hotel and wanted nothing so much as to be in that bed.

Five minutes later he walked into a lobby that had hushed down from the activity of the supper hour. In the adjacent dining-wing a swamper worked with bucket and mop; at the desk the adolescent clerk dozed. Most of the lobby chairs were empty, but Rita was in one. She sat in a far corner, curled up reading a Miles City newspaper. Lamplight laid the shadow of her long lashes upon her cheeks, and she looked like a quiet kitten, impervious to his appraisal. He had had a hectic evening, and her peacefulness was an irritation to him. He looked about for Dan Saxon and found him at a corner table with two other men, poker chips before them and the cards spread out.

Saxon raised his bandaged hand in salute and called, "Want to sit in for some poker?"

A sudden thought jarred Kittredge, and he walked over and said, "Lift your gun from leather, Saxon, and lay it down. I want a look at it."

Saxon's long face showed a faint puzzlement in the light of a bracketed lamp. "You'll have to help yourself," he said. "I can handle the pasteboards, but I can't curl my fingers around a gun butt. Not with this bandage."

Kittredge shook his head and said musingly, "You wouldn't have worked from cover, anyway."

Saxon said, understanding now showing in his eyes, "We heard shooting out on the street about an hour ago. Is that why you're looking for a gun?"

Kittredge said, "It was a sneak gun. I owe you an apology. Consider it made."

Laughter wrinkles gathered about Saxon's eyes. "Do you want to talk riddles, or do you want to play poker?"

Kittredge shook his head again. "Not tonight."

"A friendly game for small stakes," Saxon said, an edge of insistence to his voice.

"I'm no hand at cards."

"Well," Saxon said, his smile a challenge with an edge of contempt to it, "I tried my luck at *your* game."

Kittredge kicked out a chair and straddled it. "Deal me in," he said. But at once he was sorry for this decision and felt tricked; in a game of words he had let himself be bested by Saxon. He thought of the bed upstairs and sighed. He thought of the dark alley and the futile quest and inched his chair about until he could put his back to the wall.

Saxon inclined his head toward the other two players. "This is Barney Shay, who runs the mercantile, and George, his clerk. Gentlemen, I give you Reb Kittredge."

Shay was silver-haired and bloodless and looked like a New England tradesman whose roots still stuck in that far soil; George was young and sallow and probably dying of consumption. Kittredge gave them a nod; and Shay peered over his steel-rimmed spectacles and asked, "Any kin to the Cincinnati Kittredges? You know, the dealers for Colt's gun since way back?"

Kittredge grinned. "If there's a relationship, it's a business one. They peddle the gun; I sell the smoke."

Shay was humorless. "I get my stock from Babcock and Miles of Billings. Pay cash and take the discount, I always say."

Saxon said, "Cards, gentlemen?" and passed Kittredge a stack of chips, then collected the loose cards and shuffled them. Saxon's hands fascinated Kittredge, for those hands were doing that for which they were best fitted. Saxon handled the cards with a caress; the bandage seemed to bother him not at all; his hands were like sunlight flashing on the leaves of cottonwoods; they had a poetry of motion that was a delight to the eye. Saxon dealt, gave Kittredge his smile again, and said, "The chips cash in at two bits each."

Kittredge picked up his cards, thinking, *What the hell! You shoot at the man in the afternoon and play penny ante with him in the evening.* The irony of this struck him, restoring his good humor.

He won the first hand; the next two went to Barney Shay. George had a turn then, and Saxon raked in a pot or two. It was that kind of game, see-sawing across the table with no man having any high moment and the whole thing dull and listless. It might have been bunkhouse poker, a mere passing of time, except that it lacked the gusto and the camaraderie. Shay played with a grim intentness, worthy of higher stakes, and spoke no more than was necessary for the game. George was as taciturn, and Kittredge soon saw him as the shadow of his employer in all things. Only those flashing hands of Dan Saxon kept Kittredge interested. His eyes got heavy, and he wished again that he was in bed, but the game dragged on to the soft sound of chips clinking and the cards being slapped against the table top.

"Drinks, gentlemen?" Saxon asked once, but he looked only at Kittredge. "I can send for a bottle."

"No, thanks," Kittredge said.

After a while Rita folded her newspaper and came from her far corner and stood at her father's shoulder, watching the play. She soon tired of standing and took a chair near by, waiting out the game with quiet patience. Kittredge, watching her from a corner of his eye, felt the impact of her presence and wondered how many evenings she had spent this way. His own father's weakness had been the jug, and he, too, remembered nights of waiting.

At eleven o'clock, Shay yawned. He removed his spectacles and polished them with a bandanna. "That's enough for me, Dan," he said.

Saxon's face turned bland. "You owe me two dollars and six bits, Barney. I'll take it out in trade."

Shay frowned. "Sorry about what I had to tell you today. Business is business."

"And mine will be cash," Saxon said, showing no rancor.

George stood up, and the payoff was made, and

when the two had gone, Shay giving Kittredge a
short nod and George a shorter one, Saxon picked up
the cards and began idly shuffling them. He looked
like a man more asleep than awake; his eyelids were
heavy and his actions slow; yet strong in Kittredge
was the feeling that Saxon wished to prolong the
evening. Kittredge pushed himself forward on his
chair, making this first move of departure.

"Cigar?" Saxon offered and produced one from his
pocket.

Kittredge shook his head and fished out the
makings.

"Rita tells me you'd like a ranch of your own,"
Saxon said casually.

All that had transpired between him and Rita in
the room above crossed Kittredge's mind, and his
flashing thought was, *What else did she tell you,
mister?* But he only said, "A ranch? Who wouldn't?"

"Circle-S crowds up against the western hills,"
Saxon said. "You'd like the place. We've got water
and timber and good graze, and the stock is blooded.
None of your longhorn strain. The buildings are old,
but they're in good shape. The land is patented, but
there's an indebtedness against the spread. With luck,
this season could pay that off. Would such a ranch
interest you, Kittredge?"

"At what price?" Kittredge asked.

"At the cut of the cards."

Suspicion flared through Kittredge's sluggishness,
leaving him thoroughly awake. "I heard what that
storekeeper told you. Is your back that tight against
the wall?"

Saxon, too, was no longer sleepy or pretending to be. His actor's face was tight with strain. "I'm a gambling man, mister. I've let you in for a dull evening, but I can put an exciting finish to it. We cut the cards. This deck, or a new one if you prefer. High card and you own Circle-S."

Excitement stirred in Kittredge, but suspicion was still there. "Your kind never made it easy for my kind," he said. "What if it's low card?"

"Then you go to work for me at forty a month. You'll be my man, not Gault Telford's."

Rita came out of her chair and to the table. She stood at her father's shoulder, her eyes showing both amazement and fright. "No, Dad!" she cried.

Dan Saxon looked up at her, his face showing calm in the lamplight. "I tried my way; you tried yours. What else is left? Think, girl! What can we lose, really?" Kittredge had the feeling that Saxon was trying hard to convey some sort of message to her, and he saw her face pucker as she tried to understand.

But she only said, "I don't like it!"

Saxon looked hard at Kittredge. "Will you try such a gamble?"

Kittredge said, "I was told tonight that the Saxons never cheat." His lips quirked with a studied contempt. "I've watched your hands, Saxon. You could make that deck do anything you wanted."

"Perhaps," Saxon said, and his smile again held a challenge. "Must you have a sure thing?"

In Kittredge then was no willed thought; he was a wary man suddenly shed of wariness; he was a practical man gone crazy. He'd known this Dan Saxon a very few hours, and he'd bested the man at their first meeting, but now he was possessed of the strange feeling that there could be no besting Saxon, really. There was something in the man that could be budged no more than a mountain could be budged, a kind of strength that was greater than gun or fist or the money of a Gault Telford. He knew now that Saxon was bringing to its conclusion a plan that had had its beginning in Saxon's first studied insistence that he, Kittredge, sit in on a penny ante game. Step by step, this past hour had been engineered to bring them to this moment; probably the proffered whisky was to have made Reb Kittredge reckless.

Fully knowing this, he said hoarsely, "Shuffle those cards."

Saxon obeyed, his hands flashing again in the lamplight.

Kittredge found his Durham sack in his hand, the quirly still unmade; he stuffed the tobacco back in his pocket. He looked up at Rita and said, "*You* cut the deck."

She was a ghost of a girl, the color gone from her face, the hope gone from her eyes. She looked older than Cora Dufrayne; she looked harder than Cora. She was like one poised on the brink of a precipice, held fascinated and not daring to step. Then she steeled herself; Kittredge saw her fetch up courage by a force of will. She reached out and cut the deck and let it lie.

Saxon lighted up his cigar and studied the thin spiral of blue smoke. He said in an even voice, "You first, Mr. Kittredge," and was the calmest one of all.

Kittredge reached and cut quickly, exposing the five of spades. "A black-hearted card," he said.

"And a low one," Saxon observed. "I think I can beat it, friend."

He reached and made his cut, and Kittredge thought in wonder, *Everything he's ever worked for! All he owns—all his years!* It must take one kind of courage for dying, another for this kind of living. Saxon flipped over a card carelessly, exposing the three of diamonds. He looked at the card and drew hard on his cigar, the smoke writhing about his face; he touched the card with the tip of one finger; and in that breathless moment, Rita sobbed.

Saxon looked across the table at Kittredge and said, "It seems, friend, that you own a ranch."

"Yes," Kittredge said. "I own a ranch. I've beat you, and you've beat Gault Telford. That's what you were trying to get across to your girl when you told her there was nothing to lose."

"Exactly," Saxon said.

Kittredge stood up. He was aware of Rita's still presence, but he hadn't the heart to look at her. He said, "Just one question. High card would have given you the ranch—and me. Out on the street you said never to takes aces in another man's game. I was remembering that. I still think you could have made that deck dance to your tune. Why didn't you do it?"

Saxon smiled and held up his right hand so that the bandage showed. "Remember? I'm not so honest a man, I'm just a clumsy man tonight."

Chapter Seven: THE ARROWHEAD

IN THE MORNING, Kittredge was a sour man who had
not slept well. Mindful of that attempt to murder
him, he'd locked his door and propped a chair under
the knob and taken the extra precaution of strewing
crumpled papers about the floor to warn him against
any intruder. The Miles City paper Rita had discarded in the lobby had served for that. Looking at
the littered floor, he reflected that he had not been
saved from wild dreaming and fitful slumber. There
would come a time, he promised himself, when he
would sleep for a million years. That would be one
of his rewards at the end of the trail of his choosing.

Shaved, he looked at Sleeping Cat from the hotel
window, seeing a town just awakening. The buildings stood stark and harsh by daylight and were not
pleasing to him. Across the way, George showed on
Barney Shay's porch, busy with a broom; from one
of the saloons an ancient swamper limped to empty
a scrub bucket into the street. Gone were the many
men who'd crowded the boardwalks the night before.
Sleeping Cat might have been yon drunk who
squatted against a wall, a tired old man listlessly holding his head, a weary one, jaded and sick.

Gault Telford showed below, walking carefully
toward the hotel to vanish from Kittredge's range of
vision as he entered the building. Kittredge wondered if Telford had come to see him, but when no
knock sounded, he concluded that Telford was taking his breakfast. Remembering last night and the

cut of the cards and how that news would strike Telford, he began shaking with inward laughter.

The first bonneted shoppers appeared below; two of them turned into Shay's mercantile. A wagon wheeled slowly along, a man hunched on the seat, his crossed suspenders showing to Kittredge. On the side of Shay's place was tacked a huge tin sign with a colored picture showing two petticoated, aproned housewives smilingly attempting to lift a flour barrel which was labeled *Best in the World*. Kittredge thought, *Somebody ought to give 'em a hand*. Christopher Farrell came walking along, dressed in the dark suit he'd worn yesterday; and Kittredge recognized him. A crisp man, Farrell. A brand new twenty-dollar bill of a man. Kittredge had the feeling that he could take the medico between his fingers and crinkle him.

Before the drugstore, Farrell paused to pass the time of day with the pharmacist, a bald man who wore sleeve protectors and a green eyeshade. Presently the bald one turned inside; and Farrell, stirred, perhaps, by Kittredge's steady stare, raised his eyes to the hotel window. For a moment their gazes met and held. Farrell's face turned blank; he made the smallest of nods and went on along the street.

Kittredge thought, *He hates me,* and wondered why that should be. He'd not counted Farrell into his calculations last night when he'd wanted to be sure who'd fired those bushwhack shots. He wondered about Farrell now and dismissed him as having neither the nerve nor sufficient motive.

The thought crowded upon Kittredge that now he

owned a ranch. He had slept with that thought and awakened with it, but still it held no reality; it was like something dreamed. He remembered every gun job and every bonus put in the bank; he remembered the slow years of building toward independence and could not grasp that the goal had been so easily obtained. He shook his head and was like a man moving in a sleep.

Gathering up his war sack, he went down into the lobby and paid his bill. He took breakfast in the hotel dining-room, half hoping to find Telford there and see the man's face when the truth was told, half glad to find Telford gone and with him any necessity for talk. His breakfast eaten, Kittredge went to that livery stable he'd noticed the night before and rented a horse, choosing one carefully. He did his own saddling, talking to the hostler the while, then lifted himself to leather and headed west out of Sleeping Cat.

He rode over a fair, bright land that was dew-drenched and undulating and reached to the far hills. The grass was lush here, lusher range than he'd known in Texas or Wyoming, good range with good cattle feeding upon it and only a few fences to mar its expanse. He rode easily, unhurriedly; he liked being back in a saddle again. He rode alone in the great bowl of Sleeping Cat Basin, with the sky arching above him and only a few fleecy clouds showing, the pine-stippled hills drawing ever nearer. Meadow larks made their morning music, and wild roses showed, and the spearlike leaves of soapweed, and he was glad to be done with the ugliness of the town.

Such cattle as he saw interested him. He'd been told that a few years ago you could find every kind of cattle in Montana—lean longhorns that poured up from Texas, a strain sometimes mixed with short-horn blood from Missouri herds; pilgrim or barn-yard cattle from the farms of Michigan, Minnesota, Wisconsin; cattle driven eastward out of Oregon and Washington and Idaho to overstock the ranges. But since that disastrous hard winter of five years before, the wiser operators had gone in for limited range and supplemental feeding, smaller herds and better ones. Now you found a native stock that was gold on the hoof. Kittredge liked the looks of the cattle.

He was on his way to Circle-S, and he had his directions from the livery stableman. He might have ridden out with the Saxons, for he supposed they'd be heading for the ranch this morning, but he liked being alone. Moreover, there was his ever-present resentment toward Dan Saxon, the resentment of being born too late to be a cattle king, born to a rigged world where the masters of many acres stayed masters and the lesser men rode and sweated for them. A cut of the cards had changed all that, yet the feeling was strong in him that somehow the victory had gone to Dan Saxon, who had molded him, Reb Kittredge, to his own needs.

Once Kittredge had seen a Texas cowhand fashion the clay of a creek bank into a horse. It had been no such horse as mortal man had ever ridden, but it was a horse to its creator's fancy.

Considering this, he came across the miles with the sun mounting higher until the dew was gone and the grass showed crisp and summer's full fury was on the basin. The livery-stable horse was patched with sweat, and Kittredge's shirt stuck to his shoulders. The stagecoach yesterday had made for kinder traveling. But presently Kittredge began to laugh. You met a man and swapped shots with him. You met his daughter and had her throw herself at you. Then you were cutting a deck of cards and tipping your Stetson and saying good night to the two of them, and now you were riding across your own acreage with the sweat running down your back. For now he had passed through Circle-S's gate. Within the hour he came upon the ranch buildings, a scatteration of log-and-frame structures shoved up against the base of the western hills.

He looked at these buildings, thinking, *They're mine!* But he couldn't yet grasp the reality of it. He had supposed this would be a moving moment for him. He gazed at the great, gaunt ranch house and the low, sod-roofed bunkhouse and the barns and corrals and blacksmith shop. Smoke lifted from the cookshack, but otherwise the place had a deserted air. A few saddlers stomped in the corrals, switching idly at flies; no man showed himself in the yard. He looked at all this, and it embodied a dream begun in Texas; it embodied all his seeking and all his hope. He looked, but he was conscious only that he was tired from long riding.

He stepped down from the rented horse and led it to the watering-trough, letting it drink a little at a time. He stripped the gear from the mount and turned the horse into one of the corrals and hung the

saddle over a corral pole. Then he came toward the
ranch house and climbed into the shade of the long
gallery fronting the place. He saw that the ranch-
house windows had heavy hand-fashioned shutters,
scarred and pitted. Looking closer, he found a flint
arrowhead imbedded in one. This surprised him. He
had come from Texas where the Comanches had
raided and raped and killed when the moon was full
and the desert water holes brimmed, but Indian wars
were to him part of the tales of useless old men. He
wondered if Montana still had Indian trouble, and
he frowned.

Then the door opened, and Rita stood there. She
was a brightness in the doorway; she was goodness in
the day, but to him she gave a frowning contempla-
tion that held no welcome. She said in a cool voice,
"Do you want to come in?"

He'd got such an early start that he'd supposed he
must be ahead of the Saxons. Yet Rita was here; and
when he came into the ranch house, he found Dan
Saxon awaiting him, a day's stubble on his aristocratic face. Never had Saxon looked more like a
cattle king—yet he was now a cattle king who owned
not a single cow. It was the room, the setting, that
gave Saxon his air of whang-leather grandeur; it was
a big room with hand-hewn, smoke-blackened rafters
and a huge stone fireplace at the far end. The scattered furniture, tables and chairs, had been built to
last; the room looked serviceable rather than comfortable, a place where a man could jangle his spurs.

Kittredge looked about him and said with faint
irony, "I saw the arrowhead in the shutter. You for-

got to mention Indians when you were bragging about all that went with this ranch."

Saxon said, "It's been quite a while since there was any real trouble. But the first few years we slept with loaded rifles by our bunks. The Crows used to come up from the south to steal horses, and we got little protection from the military. Some of the Sioux drifted this way after the Custer fight. More recently we've had Cree down from Canada, a tattered, starving bunch. We were burned out twice in the early days. I left that arrowhead in the shutter to remind me always to stand guard. If it isn't Indians, it's likely to be rustlers."

Kittredge looked at that schooled face and thought, *He's trying to tell me something.* But he wasn't sure what Saxon had hoped to imply. Still, Kittredge knew the thrust of compassion, thinking that here was a man who had fought to hold his own and now it was lost to him. Lock, stock, and barrel. He didn't want his sympathy to show, but it must have, for Saxon shrugged slightly and spread his hands in the way of a gambler whose luck has run against him.

"We came out to get our personal belongings," he said. "We'll be off the place before sundown."

"No," Kittredge said. "You're not going."

Saxon had shown a calm acceptance till now. His face tightened, and he said, "We want neither pity nor charity. This is your place. The county seat is fifty miles beyond Sleeping Cat, but I'll pass through there on my way out of the country. The matter of the deed can be taken care of then, making Circle-S legally yours."

Kittredge shook his head; he was now a determined man showing only harshness. "You're staying here to work for me."

Saxon's lips quirked. "That wasn't in the bargain, my friend."

Rita had taken a stand away from them, putting her back to the empty fireplace, silent as a shadow. As always, Kittredge had been conscious of her; and now her voice came to him, heavy with sarcasm. "Don't you see, Dad? He wants the tables turned. He wants the rancher working for forty a month for a change."

Kittredge flashed her a hard smile. "That's the pay. You named it yourself, girl. Last night. Remember?"

Saxon said, "We're heading for St. Louis. I have kin there who'll help me get started again."

"Not yet," Kittredge said flatly. "There's those cows to be got to the railroad camp. That's the way this place gets back on its feet and Gault Telford gets trounced. You mentioned the indebtedness last night; Telford told me about your way out. You know your stock; you know the country. I don't. So I need your kind of savvy to make the delivery to the railroad. That's why you're staying."

Saxon seated himself in a rawhide-bottomed chair. "A crew goes with the place, Kittredge. And a foreman. His name is Curly Mather. The only charity I was going to ask was that you keep my crew. Now I'll not have to beg. You need those boys, for your own benefit."

"Mather?" Kittredge repeated. "The man who

came running up after I shot you? Riders come a dime a dozen, and he didn't look too bright to me. He's loyal, but his loyalty belongs to you, and it's the stupid kind that has him disobeying orders. I'll need him and the others, but I'll need you more. You're going to stay, mister."

Saxon's face stiffened. "What makes you think so?"

"Because you want Gault Telford beat. Because that was all that was left you when you talked about cutting the cards. You were seeing this place slip through your fingers anyway, so it pleased you to have it go to a man who would buck Telford—the very man Telford had brought in to beat you. *Me*. But the game isn't won, not if Telford shows up here to claim a busted ranch. You wouldn't want that. So that's why you'll stay, mister, at forty a month and chuck. You'll stay because, as much as you likely hate me, you hate Telford more."

He looked straight at Saxon, trying to read the man, but Saxon turned an impassive face to him. Then Saxon grinned and shrugged, and this was his surrender. "You've seen through me," he admitted. "Yes, I'll stay."

"Then move your stuff to the bunkhouse," Kittredge said. "You're one of the hands now."

Saxon inclined his head toward Rita, who again held silent by the fireplace. "And her?"

"She'll have to be part of the bargain I've driven with you. I know that. She can go on being queen of the castle. Just so she keeps out of the way of working men."

Rita said in a low, angry voice, "You're absolutely

insufferable!"

Kittredge turned to her. "I spoke my piece to you last night. That was only half of it. You folks handed me a ranch on a platter, but it happens to be a mighty hot platter. Nobody's going to make me let loose of it before it cools off—not you or Gault Telford or your father or the crew that rides for this spread. Nobody! I've got a ranch now, but it won't really be mine till it's in the clear. I'll wring the last ounce of sweat from every man, dog, and horse on this spread to make that possible. You're staying here because I need your father. And for no other reason. Do I make myself clear?"

Rita looked at him and was a proud girl, stiff and remote. Then the anger left her eyes and it was replaced by a certain sadness. "I told you last night I should be sorry for you," she said. "Now I'm wondering if I shouldn't be sorry for Sleeping Cat Basin. Is Circle-S just a beginning? I think we've traded one Gault Telford for another."

The sternness left Kittredge, and he grinned. "Maybe you have," he said. "But I don't mean to be rough on the ladies. Haven't you learned that by now?"

She colored, and he faced Dan Saxon again. "Tell me how the work's coming."

"We've been making an off-season gather," Saxon said. "It amounts to a fall roundup held early. It will be finished in a couple of weeks; the crew's out working at it now. From that gather we'll cut prime beef, because the grading-crew contractor demands the best. Then we'll trail it to the construction camp."

"How far to where the crew is working? I want to talk to them."

"You won't have to ride out. They're bedding the gather so close to the ranch that we haven't been using a chuck wagon. They'll be coming in for their noon meal any time now."

"I'll be waiting," Kittredge said.

It was cool here in the semidarkness of this big room, and it was a pleasant place when a man got used to the size of it. Yet he was wholly uncomfortable; he felt that he was an interloper, and also that he had been harsher than necessary.

He strode out to the gallery and stood there, putting his shoulder to a porch support and fashioning up a cigarette. He looked beyond the yard to the flatland at the base of the hills, watching for the dust cloud that would be the first sign of approaching riders. But his thoughts were elsewhere. Something nagged at his consciousness, something having to do with that Indian arrowhead and what Dan Saxon had tried to tell him without putting it directly into words.

He finished his quirly and ground it under his heel, then got out his jackknife and went to the shutter and dug out the arrowhead. It lay on his palm, an ugly reminder of savagery. He turned it over and rubbed a thumb across the rough flint surface. No hunting-arrow this, but one made for war, one made for the biggest game of all. Then he frowned and flung the arrowhead far out into the yard. He saw it strike against the watering-trough and carom.

Just then the crew came riding up.

There were six of them, and he guessed that a couple more would have been left with the gathered beef, making at least eight in all. The old ones, the grizzled ones, were Texans, men who'd come up the long trail with Saxon, he supposed. The younger ones had a salty look to them, too. He weighed them and measured them with his glance, wanting to know how much leather was in them, wanting to know how they'd stand when Telford made a play. He judged them to be fighting men, all, and was pleased.

Then they were into the yard, stirring up a maelstrom of dust as they came to a stop; some stepped down from their saddles. He recognized Curly Mather, remembering him from their brief encounters in Sleeping Cat. He saw that Mather recognized him, too, for Mather tossed his reins to one of the younger men and came toward the gallery frowning.

Kittredge was at once wary and at once ready, knowing instantly that here was the one who would give him trouble.

Chapter Eight: GIRL IN THE SADDLE

DAN SAXON CAME OUT OF THE HOUSE and stood behind Kittredge's right shoulder; Kittredge was conscious of his being there and knew an habitual squeamishness at having a man behind his back. He listened to the soft scrape of Saxon's boot soles on the porch and reflected that Saxon might have come to regret the bargain of the cards. Thus he was acutely aware that he was now whipsawed between Saxon and Saxon's crew. Dan Saxon was a sharp one who would see the shape of opportunity. This sorry knowledge put a tension in Kittredge and a feeling of having been careless. He was all wolf in this moment, smelling the trap.

But Saxon, scarcely raising his voice, said, "Boys, this is Reb Kittredge, the new owner, up out of Johnson County. You'll be taking your orders from him." He threw the words out to the crew and let them lie.

Curly Mather stopped in mid-stride, his face lifted to the porch. He stood peering from under his hat-brim, a tall man, tall almost as Kittredge, a slab-muscled man, a weather-burned man, the product of a hard era, a hard way of life. His solid features showed his astonishment; he had the look of not believing what his ears had told him. He spoke quickly, his voice truculent. "The hell you say."

Edgy, Kittredge thought. *Talks first and thinks afterward,* and he knew how Mather must be handled.

Saxon said, "Sorry, Curly, but it's so."

The rest of the crew waited, those who hadn't already dismounted coming down from saddles and forming a solid body behind Mather to make restless movements of hands and feet. From Mather they took their day's orders; to Mather they gave loyalty and obedience, and these things were ingrained and had become tradition, a part of cattledom. To them Curly Mather was now a weather vane, and they would turn whichever way the wind blew him. This, too, Kittredge recognized; and he looked at the old, guarded faces and the young, taut faces and knew that the things they understood were the hard hand and the quick quirt. They were a leathery breed that prized its independence and recognized only the rawest strength; he knew them full well, for he had been born to their breed.

That was why he said, "Nothing's changed, boys. You've got the same job with the same brand at the same pay. You'll find me a square boss if you give me a square shake. Now get your grub and get back to work." All the while a question was nagging at him. Why had Saxon made it a point to mention Johnson County?

Mather's face stayed unyielding. "I'm not working for any damn gun slick!"

Ready for this, Kittredge cleared the gallery steps without touching them. He made the jump and lunged across the openness to Mather so suddenly as to give the foreman no warning. He came at Mather with his right fist looping up; his knuckles struck hard at Mather's jaw. Too late, Mather saw the blow coming and pulled his head aside. Kittredge's fist glanced off Mather's shoulder, but Mather's wild defensive move threw the foreman off balance, and he went down. Kittredge towered over him, putting his boot against Mather's chest, pinning Mather down.

Kittredge said through his teeth, "You're a hired man, Mather. I've seen your kind on every bedbug-crawling two-bit spread between the Rio and the Yellowstone. You'll never be anything but a hired man. You can work for me, or you can ride out. Now get to your feet and make up your mind!"

He stepped back from Mather, and the man put

the heel of his hand to the ground and levered himself upward to an awkward stand. Death was in his eyes; they held Kittredge and tore him to pieces, and Kittredge was sure that Mather was going for his gun. The decision stood out on Mather for an instant and then was gone. Now Kittredge understood why Saxon had mentioned Johnson County and was grateful to Saxon. Mather's stare shifted beyond Kittredge to the gallery.

Kittredge asked, "Well, are you staying?"

Mather was still staring beyond Kittredge, staring, Kittredge supposed, at Dan Saxon. Kittredge wanted mightily to turn his head, but he knew better. Only as long as he faced Mather could he hope to dominate Mather. And Mather, cooled off for any gun fighting by the knowledge that he faced a professional of proved standing, was now making another fight with himself; it showed in his face.

Mather said then, "I'll stay."

Kittredge said, "If there's anything still stuck in your craw, get it out!"

Mather's face worked. "Just don't ever lay a hand on me again!"

"That will be up to you," Kittredge said. His glance moved from Mather to the men behind the foreman; his eyes were brittle and compelling, showing no charity. "Anybody else got anything to say?"

Again there was that restless movement of hands and feet, and the animosity that rose from the bunch made its impact against Kittredge. When he had humbled Mather, he had humbled all of them and earned their hatred; by this same token Mather had answered for all of them. That was the way of it. Someone made a move to lead a horse toward the corrals. Another followed him, and another, their boots scuffing dust, and thus they signified their intent; they would stick.

Mather was the last to move away. He gave Kittredge the fullness of his malevolence in a final glance and headed stolidly across the yard. Only then did Kittredge look toward the gallery. Dan Saxon stood there, a silent spectator to what had happened, his face showing nothing, though some secret laughter sharpened his eyes. Beside him stood Rita, come quietly from the house.

Kittredge smiled up at her. "So it was you told Mather to stay."

Rita's lips were tight. "I told him nothing," she said. "But if I'd nodded my head, he'd have ridden out. I like it better that he's staying. If there's one man on the ranch who'll cut you down to size, it's Curly. Sooner or later you'll push him too far."

"Maybe," Kittredge said.

He faced about again, taking a hipshot stand and watching the crew drift from the corrals to the cookshack. He remembered that he was very hungry, and he walked to the cookshack, waited his turn and gave his face a *whoosh* from the washbasin on the bench outside the door. He had a look at himself in a distorted mirror tacked to the cookshack wall, flattened out his hair with the heels of his hands, and walked inside.

He found most of the crew seated around a long table, Mather among them. The cook was filling plates; and Kittredge sized him up and saw him to be gray as a badger and cantankerous but sound of limb, and judged that he would be an additional fighting man in a pinch. Telford, who'd tried to hire a Reb Kittredge, would likely hire others; and some dark night Telford would strike at Circle-S.

An empty chair stood at the head of the table, and Kittredge knew this must be Dan Saxon's. Saxon and Rita entered, and Kittredge became conscious that every eye was on him, waiting to see if he had usurped Saxon in all things. Their antagonism would be sharpened if he, Kittredge, took that chair. This gave him a hard choice; he had shown them a firm hand and he must continue to do so, but he needed their friendship.

He walked to the head of the table, got behind the chair and hauled it out, making a gesture of this. He looked at Rita. "Sit down," he invited.

For a moment she hesitated, not knowing how to interpret his act; Kittredge kept his face bland. She smiled, and grew prettier; she came to the chair and let him seat her, and she whispered, "Thanks."

He bent to her ear. "Why not?" he asked, low-voiced. "You kept the crew here for me."

Anger flushed her cheeks. "I did nothing for *you!* Please understand that!"

He wondered at his own perverseness that drew him toward this girl yet kept him always at odds with her. He had stripped her of a home, and she had met that disaster with courage, and he could re-spect her for it. He supposed that the resentment he harbored against her was like that he felt toward

Dan Saxon; she was one who'd lived in ease because of an accident of circumstance, and he'd always hated her kind. Yet now, with the fragrance of her hair strong in his nostrils and her rigid shoulders within reach of his hand, he was strangely stirred; he was a hungry man at the feast.

But he said, keeping a straight face, "If you want to shoot me, I'll loan you my gun."

"I'll leave that job for someone who'll do it well."

"Then be sure to dance at my funeral," he said.

He found an empty chair for himself and fell to eating, showing a healthy man's appetite. Outwardly he paid no heed to the crew, yet he was keenly alert; and he noticed that the talk was stiff and desultory, with none of the usual camaraderie of a ranch meal. He took to studying the crew and began now to see them as individuals, and he caught a name occasionally. There was a Larry and a Frank and a Pecos. Once he looked across at Dan Saxon, who was seated opposite him; Saxon's face was poker-stiff, but the glint of laughter was still in his eyes.

After the meal, Kittredge drifted out into the yard with the crew, cut out a Circle-S horse from the corral, and put a saddle on it. He paid strict attention to this task, knowing they were watching him and knowing, too, that their measure of him would in part be made by how he handled himself. A gun hand they would hate; a good cowhand they would appreciate. When Mather and the others rode out, he rode with them.

They paralleled the hills, moving southward for a mile and more over rolling country, and shortly they came upon the beef gather, a great brown blotch upon the grass. A couple of men squatted in the skimpy shade of their ground-anchored horses, watching. At a nod from Mather, these two rose to leather and headed toward the ranch headquarters for their noon meal.

Kittredge rode close to Mather, dragged out the makings and fashioned up a cigarette, then offered the Durham sack to the foreman. Mather shook his head.

"How's it coming?" Kittredge asked.

Mather's lips thinned down, but he spoke in a civil voice. "We've combed most of the draws. Another two weeks and we'll start cutting out the stuff we're trailing to the railroad. The boys know their job and they know the country. If you want to see how we operate, trail along with anyone you choose."

He rode away from Kittredge and began giving orders to the men; at once there was a great show of confusion, but out of the seeming chaos came orderly activity. Two men were delegated to stay with the herd, spelling the two who'd headed to the ranch. This pair went to a wagon and got firewood from it and started building a branding-fire. Their job would be to brand and earmark the summer calves that had come since the spring roundup. The others got fresh horses from the small, rope-corraled *remuda* and began to diverge, the riders spreading fanwise to cover a wide arc of surrounding country.

Kittredge nudged his horse and attached himself to an old-timer, a grizzled one who rode southward until the herd was lost from sight. The oldster headed into a draw. Kittredge trailed silently behind him. When the draw split, two brushy, wooded thumbs digging at angles into the hill, the oldster pulled up. He was a man to Kittredge's liking; he had about him the free spirit of limitless spaces; he had a puckered face that somehow contrived to look as wise as a coyote's and as stolid as a cow's. He cocked a bright-blue eye at Kittredge.

"Be you a cowboy?"

Kittredge nodded. "Starting today."

"I'm Pecos," said the old-timer.

"I know; I caught it at the table. It's a good name."

Pecos showed neither affability nor antagonism; if he had made his judgment of Kittredge, he was keeping it to himself. "I'll take this here right-hand draw," he said. "You want to help, you find yourself any cows that's up the other draw, then chouse 'em toward the bedding-ground."

Kittredge crooked a leg around his saddle horn. "At a walk? Or shall I run hell out of 'em?"

Pecos squinted hard, but Kittredge kept his face free of guile. Pecos grinned, and with that grin a friendship was forged. "You go to hell," Pecos said with great cheerfulness and headed up the right-hand draw.

Whereupon Kittredge rode alone, following the draw in its gentle climb upward. Chokecherry grew here, and wild plum, and on the rockier slopes hackberry showed. Here was rugged country that reminded him of the Texas *brasada*. Another mile into the hills, Kittredge came upon three steers bearing the Circle-S brand. He got these to drifting down the draw and rode on. He found himself liking this work; it was like going back to a remembered place and thereby dissolving all the years since he'd last looked upon it. He liked the sky over him and the saddle leather under him; he liked the demand upon a skill he had long forsaken. He grew prideful of the task and lost himself in it.

When the draw sprouted fingers, he explored each one meticulously and found a couple more steers which he started downhill, being careful not to run the tallow off them. Damn but Pecos's jaw had dropped when he'd put that silly question to him! He rode along thinking about this and chuckling; and then, in the far reaches, he found a mossy-horn, an ancient bunch-quitter that had eluded many roundups and grown wild as any wolf. He caught the flash of reddish-brown hide in a thicket and heard the crash of brush, and the chase was on.

Kittredge was glad he was aboard a Circle-S horse rather than the livery-stable mount. The horse had savvy, but the mossy-horn was elusive, and the pursuit led through pine thickets and deeper brush and called for all of Kittredge's riding skill. Presently he found himself cussing that perverse steer with considerable heat. The chase became a challenge to him; at last he got a rope snapping at the rump of the mossy-horn, heading him downhill; but here was a born bunch-quitter, quick to turn at any time; and he herded it out of many corners before he descended to the place where he had parted from Pecos.

It was then the accident happened.

The scrap of paper might have come from a letter

some cowhand had dropped, or it might have been the label from a can. It had caught on a bush, and Kittredge hadn't noticed it on the ride up, but now it fluttered in the breeze. Kittredge's horse laid back its ears, shied, and caught him unprepared. He tried frantically to clamp leather with his knees and turn his toes inward to lock himself in the saddle; and then, in a wild moment of realization that he was off balance, he kicked free of the stirrups. He hit the ground hard, but he contrived to land on his shoulder and at once rolled away from the rearing horse. But the steer turned and came at him.

Again he was caught unprepared. A longhorn would inevitably charge an unhorsed rider, but this was native stock, a gentler breed. But this steer was coming on with lowered head. Kittredge tried to get at his gun, but his holster had been twisted awry by the fall. His hand clawed futilely, and he had then the thrusting knowledge that he was doomed. There was no fear in this; there was no time for fear. He was on one knee, a frantic, struggling man, when a rider cut between him and the steer, snapping at the mossy-horn with a rope end, turning the brute.

Pecos! he thought and was weak with relief.

He got up, caught at the reins of his horse, and was at once into the saddle, and safe. He saw then that the rider was Rita—Rita in jeans and sombrero and denim brush jacket, her eyes big with excitement. He neck-reined his horse toward hers and said, "What the hell are you doing out here?"

She had got the steer loping down the trail. She drew up beside Kittredge and said, "Earning my keep. I've choused out seven cows this afternoon. How well have you done?" She was breathing hard; her face, flushed by exertion, was startlingly alive, startlingly pretty.

He shook his head. "It's no game for a girl."

"I've ridden in roundups before! Whenever I chose to. You told Dad this morning why you were keeping *him*. I was supposed to be a free boarder who went along with the bargain. You have your kind of pride, friend, but you never stop to think that other people have theirs. If I eat Circle-S grub, I do Circle-S work."

He plucked that fluttering bit of paper from the bush and balled it tightly in his fist. "You saved my life," he said.

"Anybody—Curly, even—would have done the same under the circumstances."

"I wonder," he said.

She wheeled her horse about. "We're wasting time. There are cows to be gathered."

Then she was spurring down the trail, gone about her work. He watched her ride away; he watched until a bend of the draw took her from his sight; and he said softly, aloud, "Well, I'll be damned!"

Then he threw back his head, and his laughter came and was caught by the hills and sent echoing.

Chapter Nine: CORA

To CORA DUFRAYNE, the passing days in Sleeping Cat brought a certain routine that held for her both pandemonium and peace. By night she sang her songs and so belonged to blue tobacco smoke and a tinkling piano and the wild bedlam of men tasting the pleasures of the Bagdad. She hated the nights. But the days were hers, the long dreamy sun-lit days while Sleeping Cat stirred languidly outside her window; and the only sounds rising from the barroom were the scrape of the swamper's mop, the soft talk of men doing lazy drinking, the slap of cards in listless, time-killing games. She slept late, for her last song was often sung at three or four in the morning, and sometimes she lay long in bed, watching the play of sunlight on the carpeting, finding in this a feline luxury. All the hours were hers thereafter until the first cue came in the early evening.

Sometimes she sewed, seating herself by the window so she might watch the eternally shifting tableaux of the street below; sometimes she read. As much as possible, she avoided going out, except that she took her evening meal in the hotel dining-room, and sometimes, growing tired of the Bagdad, she took an afternoon stroll, a parasol tipped over her shoulder and her skirts swishing along the boardwalks. These strolls always meant running a gantlet of speculative-eyed men, who either showed her too much politeness or none at all, and housewives who turned their faces from her. She had known such inspections and such aloofness in other towns and grown impervious; but still she kept largely to her room, centering her life there.

She was not consciously lonely. She had long ago learned to draw on inner resources. And often one or another of the percentage girls would drift in during the afternoon to sit, pallid without paint, and recount the little joys and tragedies of their existences. One had danced with a cowboy who'd smiled and made gallant talk, hinting that he would like such a one as she for wife. "You be nice to him," Cora had counseled, knowing that on the woman-starved frontiers many a first family had been founded by just such alliances. Another girl had had a letter from a distant and nearly-forgotten home town and wept over it in the night. To all these girls Cora gave of her patience and her time, feeling infinitely older than they.

The swamper had been assigned to clean her room daily, but she'd found his efforts far short of perfection and had taken over the task herself. She delighted in this, for she was an inherently neat person and inherently feminine; and on this certain afternoon as she worked with a dustcloth, she caught herself smiling with the thought that she might have made some man a good wife. This turned her mind to Reb Kittredge.

He often crowded her consciousness in the hours that were hers alone, and she wondered what had become of him since that night when she'd made him two offers and had both spurned. From the free talk of the saloon, she'd learned much about the basin and its people, but no man had had news of Kittredge. She had even asked Gault Telford, but he had shrugged and given no answer. But Kittredge was not so easily dismissed from her mind. She looked now at that chair he had straddled while she'd trusted him with the full truth about herself. She re-

membered that gaunt, saturnine face and wondered
if she were in love with him and found this a startling thought. She'd never been in love, and she
fancied that Kittredge hadn't, either. She wondered
whether so free a spirit as his would be gentled by
love or made more rebellious by its shackles.

She thought then of her ambition, akin to his own.
They could have done so very much together! She
had with the passing days seen no way to further
her scheme to snatch from Gault Telford that which
he had snatched from others; and sometimes she'd
despaired, knowing the limitations of a woman in
a man's game. She had needed Kittredge's help so
badly, and strong in her was the conviction that he
would come back, drawn by one or the other of the
offers she'd made him. This surety, she told herself, was not vanity; it was merely that they were
alike, she and Kittredge, and some day he would
see that. In the meantime, hers was the patient way,
and she could only bide her time. Her goal was fixed,
and in some vagrant moment opportunity would
present itself. This, also, she believed firmly.

And now there was a knocking at the door; and
she opened it to find Gault Telford standing there,
scrupulously neat, as always. He had been so strong
in her thoughts just a moment before that she had
a sweeping sense of guilt, a feeling that her scheming had somehow reached through to him, summon-
ing him here to denounce her.

But he only said, smiling, "May I come in?"

She'd been told by the percentage girls that it was
his habit to burst through doors without knocking,

and she'd been prepared to reprimand him sternly if he intruded upon her in such a manner. This she had not found necessary. It was as though he'd learned his lesson elsewhere; for on his infrequent visits he had always come like this, showing a careful politeness. She made a gesture, welcoming him; and he came inside with that peculiarly light way of walking that was his.

Looking about him, he asked, "Is everything going well with you?"

"I've no complaints," she said. "Won't you sit down, please."

He did so, and she took a stand before him and was conscious of the picture she made, tall and statuesque and handsome, trained to whet the desires of men. Her pose had the naturalness of long practice, yet she felt that it was wasted on Telford. She had from the first looked for the chink in his armor and found none. Those sensual lips were a lie, for he'd shown no interest other than a commercial one in any of the girls at the Bagdad. A saloon owner, he took nothing but beer at his own bar. He was a man impervious to all ordinary temptations; he had a peculiar kind of strength she'd found in no other man. Whatever had brought him here today dealt with dollars and cents.

Knowing this, she said in her straightforward manner, "What is it you wish of me?"

Behind his thick glasses, his eyes held their perpetual amusement, yet she sensed that he was gravely concerned, driven here by trouble.

He said, "You asked me a question the other day.

I've since found the answer. I've learned that your friend Reb Kittredge is working for Circle-S. As a common cowhand."

"I don't believe it!" she said.

He shrugged. "I sent one of the housemen to scout the place with field glasses. He saw Kittredge at work."

This was as startling to her as hearing that a grizzly bear had been tamed for the saddle. She shook her head. "I've learned a lot about the Sleeping Cat country. What you say doesn't make sense. You brought Kittredge in to finish off a certain Dan Saxon. That's common knowledge. So is the fact that Saxon is broke. The only thing that would have swung Kittredge from your side to Saxon's is the offer of bigger pay. Saxon obviously couldn't have made such an offer. What then would hold a man like Kittredge at Circle-S?"

Telford smiled and got up from the chair and moved over to the draped window. He stood peering down at the street for a long time, and then he said, "Here she is now. Come and take a look for yourself."

Cora came to the window and stood at Telford's shoulder, and thus she had her first look at Rita Saxon. Rita had apparently come to town to do a bit of shopping, for she had a package under her arm. She walked along, a vibrant, olive-skinned girl with a sultry Spanish beauty that made the street brighter. Cora saw that fluid grace to her movements, that promise of passion in her full lips, and knew that yonder was a girl who could move a man—

even such a man as Reb Kittredge.

She asked, "Who is she?"

"Saxon's daughter, Rita. I happen to know that she visited Kittredge at the hotel the first night he was here. You see, she asked the desk clerk the number of his room, and that was reported to me. Two and two are four, Cora. How else was Kittredge bought away from me?"

Silence held her for a stricken moment. Then: "I still don't believe it!" she said, but her glance was on Rita, and her certainty was shaken.

Telford spread his hands. "You recall the night I heard you sing in Miles City and hired you to come here? You made me a wise little speech about how men most desire the unattainable. Every man has his particular weakness. Now you've just seen Kittredge's. A girl who wouldn't wipe her feet on him."

"No!" she cried. "Not Kittredge. He wouldn't be swayed by any woman."

Telford smiled broadly. "I recall that he visited you here that same night. After he'd seen Rita Saxon. Tell me, was your charm as great as hers?"

She turned on him, all tigress; she raised her hand to claw at him, but something in his magnified eyes stopped her, that and the realization of a truth. Her kind of woman had never been able to compete against the Rita Saxons. And there was the fact that Kittredge had shown her, Cora, a resistance beyond shaking. She had had her wild dream that Kittredge would come back to her, and that dream was now ashes at her feet. She saw herself suddenly as a woman scorned, and fury made her face hard. She willed herself against open anger, not wanting to give Telford whatever satisfaction he'd hoped for in this moment.

She said in a voice that shook only slightly, "If he was fool enough to sell out at that price, he's welcome to her."

"Ah," Telford said, "but we're ahead. We know his weakness."

She turned away. "It's no concern of mine."

"I am a businessman, Cora," Telford said. "I'm here to talk business. What has happened is not to my liking. I tell you this frankly. I have worked hard to get a hold on the basin, but in many cases I hold only options against the ranches. I know there is dissatisfaction. Dan Saxon has held out against me, and that has started other ranchers thinking. With Kittredge siding Saxon, my whole house of cards might come down. I must do something about Kittredge. So far as I know, you're the only friend he has in town. I think you could get him here."

Her interest quickened. "You want me to persuade him to go on your payroll?"

He shook his head; his eyes now were feral. "I trust no man twice. I want him in this room, with a gun waiting beyond the doorway. When he is packed out of here dead, there'll be a thousand dollars bonus for you."

She had turned very still, not wanting her wild thinking to show. She'd hoped for an opportunity that would leave Telford open, and the opportunity was here, come so suddenly as to astonish her. She said in a small, tight voice, "And who would handle the gun?"

"Ah," he said, "that's a question. His reputation scares all of them."

"And if I could name you men who want a chance against Kittredge? Men who would come into town willingly to do the job if they could be promised the protection you might give them?"

His eyes gleamed. "Another thousand tacked to the bonus, Cora."

"No," she said. "It's not enough. Not nearly enough. My price is a half interest in the Bagdad."

He laughed. "Have you any idea what this place is worth?"

"Yes," she said. "I have."

He turned thoughtful, his eyes brightly speculative behind his glasses. He said then, slowly, "You're bringing in patronage; I think soon you'd be asking for a percentage of the profits, anyway. A quarter interest, Cora?"

Her thought was that here was her wedge, that with such a start she could drive deep. "A quarter interest," she agreed. "I must have it in writing."

"This very afternoon."

"Then," she said, "I'll trust you. Can you find three brothers named Jimson?"

"I know them," he said. "Buck and Lonny and Pete. Yes, I can find them. I can find any man in the basin. But the Jimsons are stupid, not the kind for this job."

"There are three of them," she said. "No man can fire three directions at once, not even Kittredge.

What you don't know is that the Jimsons have reason enough of their own to kill Kittredge. That first night, they came to Sleeping Cat looking for him. They were scared to stay, perhaps because they'd held up the stagecoach that afternoon. But you could hide them out here in town."

This also received his careful consideration. "It's worth a trial," he decided. He looked at her with new appreciation. "You're a thinking woman. I'll not regret having you as a partner. Remember, though, that I own the controlling interest."

"I'll remember," she said and kept her smile inward. "I'll expect you back in an hour with the papers."

He crossed to the door and left, and at once she found herself shaking. She supposed this should be a jubilant moment, but she recognized the anger within herself. She moved to the window and looked down at the street, but Rita Saxon was no longer in sight. She thought of Reb Kittredge and suddenly picked a vase from the teakwood table and hurled it at the closed door. The vase shattered explosively, and she looked at the scattered shards and was ashamed of her childishness.

She felt as though there was something she should be fleeing, and she couldn't put a name to it. She said aloud, "A quarter interest!" hoping for the jubilation that hadn't come. But she was empty of all feelings save one. She knew now a great regret, a sense of being tainted. And she knew there could be no escaping this, not ever.

Chapter Ten: MAN AND WOMAN

THESE WERE ROUNDUP DAYS at Circle-S—days that began to the clatter of the cook's alarm clock set on an overturned dishpan to make a greater racket, days of taking the early-morning kinks out of saddlers and combing the far draws to build the beef gather. Hard days, hot days. Rush-and-roar days. Rita rode with the crew, as did Dan Saxon of the bandaged hand, both of them turning in full measures of work.

Kittredge, softened by the remembrance that Rita had saved his life, and softened, too, by his growing admiration for her, tried finding easy chores for the girl; but she constantly saw through his scheming and defied him. Once he assigned her to be the cook's helper, only to find her in a saddle an hour later. He made a show of anger then. "The first thing you've got to learn," he insisted, "is to take orders!"

She gave him a bland, sultry look, but he could tell she was laughing at him. She said, "The cook swears he'll quit if I keep cluttering up his domain."

Convinced that Telford would soon strike, Kittredge overhauled every gun on the place to be sure it was in working order, checked the ammunition, and sent Rita to town for a fresh supply. When she balked at this errand, claiming it was only a subterfuge to keep her from the roundup, he said, "Do as you're told. If you think the chore isn't important, just try standing up against a gun with a slingshot. We need those shells."

And so the days passed. Dust rose, and the

acrid odor of singed hair and flesh was in the air, and the mingled blatting of branded calves and concerned mother cows made a constant cacophony. Saddle leather squealed, and rope ends snapped, and men grew gaunt from toil and short of temper, but still the work went on. At night while the stars stood out and the coyotes mourned in the high hills, the bedded herd lay lulled by the old Texas songs as the nighthawks rode their endless circles.

Forty a month an' chuck-wagon grub,
Forty a month and found.
Oh, think of the joys of a cowboy's life
While you're ridin' the old bed ground . . .

Kittredge took his turn at the nighthawking, and on his off nights slept at the ranch house, usurping Dan Saxon's bedroom, while Rita slept across the hall from him and her father retired to the bunkhouse with the crew.

Curly Mather raised an objection to this arrangement. "You mean you're going to keep on staying alone in the house with Rita?" he demanded of Kittredge.

They were on the gallery that evening, Rita and Kittredge and Dan Saxon, the men having an after-supper smoke; and Mather had joined them here, come to talk over tomorrow's work. Through the days he had been a tractable man who had gone about his job with efficiency, proving himself a good hand with cattle. There had been a stiff restraint in his necessary contacts with Kittredge, but not till tonight had he raised a personal issue. Mather was a good foreman, Kittredge had decided.

Now Kittredge looked at him and smiled a slow smile.

"Rita hasn't been doing me any harm."

Mather made a big, solid shape in the darkness of the gallery, belligerency in the cant of his shoulders.

"Damn it!" he snapped angrily. "That isn't what I meant."

"What did you mean?" Kittredge asked softly, then said with no rancor, "The ranch house is mine. She can keep on sleeping here if she chooses. Or she can go to the bunkhouse or the barn."

"Look," Mather argued, "in the name of common decency, it shouldn't be her that moves out of the house."

"Never mind, Curly," Rita interjected wearily. "I'll lock my door."

"Just the same," Mather said hotly, "I'm unrolling my soogans right here on the gallery. I'll be within shouting-distance if you need me, Rita."

"What happens if it's *me* that starts bellowing for help?" Kittredge asked placidly.

He'd been watching Mather closely, and he saw the man take a step forward with his fist cocked; but Rita said sharply, "Forget it, Curly!"

"I've spoke my piece," Mather said stubbornly and swung down into the yard.

Thus it came about that Mather spread his blankets on the gallery each evening thereafter, while Kittredge and Rita retired to the house. The crew, showing a cool, civil attitude toward Kittredge, made a great pretense of ignoring this nightly ritual of Mather's; but Dan Saxon sometimes smiled when, leaving the house at an evening's end, he had to step over the foreman to get from the gallery.

No more was said about the subject, but Mather was still in charge of the roundup; and whenever it was his own turn to do the nighthawk's trick, he named Kittredge as his partner, keeping the two of them away from the ranch house at the same time. They rode the long circles, passing each other in sullen silence till the watch was done.

On the other nights, Kittredge lay in the dark house, strongly conscious of Rita's nearness. He had thought her to be a cattle king's spoiled darling, and he'd resented her with the resentment he gave to all those in the high places. Now he knew she could do a day's work. She was a paradox to him; but she was also a woman, dark and smiling and making a strong call to an unnamed hunger in the stillness of the night.

Dr. Christopher Farrell, too, knew restive nights. On this particular evening he sat in the parlor of his cottage in Sleeping Cat, a man tired and troubled. Since early morning, he'd made the rounds of his patients among the basin ranchers, traversing the rough roads in his square-topped buggy. His day's work was not yet done, for a certain Mrs. Luke Walker would undoubtedly have her first baby before the sun rose again. He'd looked in on her this afternoon and found her fretful and afraid, a young thing come out of Wisconsin to be the mail-order bride of Luke Walker, who had built up a two-bit spread from nothing. Farrell had promised to drop back tonight. Now he wearily contemplated the fact that he should be on his way within the hour.

It had been a discouraging day, and in the present blackness of his mood lay the long shadow of that day. Not that his patients were doing badly. He could congratulate himself on being a good doctor, but some ills were beyond his curing. That was because of Gault Telford. Farrell had liked Sleeping Cat Basin at first, but with the passing months a change had come, and Gault Telford was behind it—Telford and his ambition to control all the basin ranches. Therein lay the shadow.

Take Luke Walker, for instance. Once Walker had shown the pride of a man building by the sweat of his brow, building toward his own independence. Now he worked for Telford as manager of the very ranch he, Walker, had wrought out of nothing. He had got a fancy down payment from Telford and the assurance of a manager's pay, all of this in a contract so involved that it had made no sense to Farrell, who'd been shown it, and less to Walker. Thus Walker had become a disheartened man, chained here by a wife and the coming child, chained to an existence governed by a piece of paper Telford had virtually forced upon him.

Walker's despair was reflected all over the basin, except, Farrell supposed, on Dan Saxon's Circle-S, the holdout ranch. And men who'd once looked hopefully toward Dan Saxon were now laying bets as to how long Saxon would last, bucking Telford alone. That was the pitiful thing; and Farrell had seen it again today, the broken spirit, the abject surrender. True, there was some talk that Reb Kittredge was now working for Saxon; and a few put faith in this, saying the tide might yet be turned. Farrell hadn't shared their optimism. Whatever Kittredge was doing, he was doing for himself.

Had Sue been here tonight, Farrell would have talked of these things to her and thus eased his worries. He missed her mightily; she had been the solid rock to which he'd always returned after his day's wanderings. The house stood empty without her, and he remembered Saxon's suggestion that he seek new fields. Now he understood what Saxon had meant. And there was the letter on the table beside him, the letter he'd found waiting when he'd driven home in the late afternoon.

He picked up the letter and looked at the signature of his friend, who'd been his classmate at medical school. The letter was from Idaho and spoke of many things, but it was the last page that Farrell now reread.

And so we are having a great deal of trouble in this Coeur d'Alene country, the culmination of what commenced last January when all the mines were closed. We've had strikes and strikebreakers, gunmen and dynamiting; and now the Governor has declared martial law and a thousand Negro troops are among us. What the end will be, I do not know.

But the point I want to make, Chris, is that

here is country with a future for a doctor. I could use a partner, or if you preferred, I'd help you get established in a practice of your own. This is rough, violent country, my friend, but I believe that a humanitarian lurks beneath that cold exterior you show the world. I could certainly use your help. That is why I say you are needed here. I do hope you will think about it.

My heartfelt respects to you and your wife, a lady I am still looking forward to meeting.

He put the letter aside and smiled an ironic smile, again remembering how he'd bared himself to Dan Saxon, admitting his cowardice. *Come to the Coeur d'Alene country, my friend! Ho, for a rough land where violence is the order of the day! You'll fit in just fine, Chris Farrell!* Sometime soon he must compose an answer to that letter; he'd not yet got around to letting his far-flung friends know of Sue's passing. Sometime he would write, but not tonight.

He grew suddenly tired of the house and was glad for work to which he could turn his hands. He got his hat and went outside. He came briskly up the street; this manner of walking was habit with him; and he paused at the livery stable where he kept his horse and found it was being grained. He left orders that the animal be hitched to the buggy as soon as possible, promised to return within half an hour, and continued walking.

Sleeping Cat was not as crowded tonight as it had been on his return from Miles City, for the construction workers descended in droves only on payday, and thus few of them were now in town. Still, the hitchrails were crowded by the horses of basin cowhands; and the saloons all seemed to be doing a good business. Noise spilled from the Bagdad, and its lamplight laid a saffron wash upon the boardwalk. On impulse he turned into the establishment and made his way to the bar.

He'd been here before but never as a patron; he'd come to sew up a broken scalp or probe for a bit of lead, and once he'd examined a percentage girl who'd developed, of all things, a case of measles. He was no teetotaler; he'd just never found any real pleasure in saloon drinking, but tonight he ordered whisky and stood studying his own face, so long and sensitive, in the bar mirror. The drink took some of the tiredness out of him. He recognized a couple of the townspeople and received their respectful nods. The blacksmith was here, a mug of beer before him; and so was George from Barney Shay's mercantile. Farrell listened to the hum of talk and grew drowsy. Presently the curtains of the stage parted, and Cora appeared and began singing.

Farrell listened, turning about and propping his elbows on the bar. That Lorena song was one Sue had liked. He watched Cora and was moved by her; he'd seen her on the street, but he'd had no real contact since that late afternoon they'd both stepped from the stagecoach. He knew now that he'd been deliberately shunning her, and he knew why this was so; his guilt had remained, deep-burning, ever since that incident of the Jimsons' holdup. And because he was tired of living with that fretful remembrance, he had his second impulse of the evening. When Cora, her act finished, ascended the stairs, he followed after her.

He was not sure which room was hers, but she'd left the door open, and he spied her. He hesitated on the threshold, strangely irritated by the opulence within; and she said, "Won't you step inside?"

He entered, removing his hat as he did so. She showed no surprise at his visit; she gestured toward one of the chairs; and when he'd gravely seated himself, she said, "I've known that sooner or later you'd come."

He said sarcastically, "Does everyone?"

A shadow crossed her face, and he was instantly sorry. "Excuse a tired and touchy man," he said.

"And a troubled one," she said. "Troubled people always come to me."

He said, with a rush of words, "There's something I have to know. That day of the holdup, you stepped forward to collect the Jimsons' guns. Why did you do that? It was a man's job."

In the lamplight, she showed surprise. "I supposed you knew. After all, I had a score to settle; they'd threatened to lay hands on me, remember. It pleased me to be the one to take their guns."

He said in vast surprise, "So that was it!" and suddenly felt like laughing. He had lived these several days with a shame she had banished in an instant.

"Yes," she said and hesitated. "Would you care for some wine?"

He was mindful that he was here on borrowed time, but looking at her, so tall and statuesque and handsome, he was loath to leave. "A rancher's wife is having her first baby tonight," he said, and got his inspiration then. "Will you come with me? It will be easier for her if there's a woman present. Could you come?"

She shook her head. "I could come, but no rancher's wife would want me."

"This one would."

She was thoughtful for a long moment, and sad. Then: "Where do you keep your buggy, Doctor?"

"At the livery stable."

"I'll have to change clothes. I'll meet you there in ten minutes."

"I'll be ready," he said and got up and moved to the door.

Not until he was downstairs and working his way toward the batwings did he understand her strategy; she'd wanted to spare him from an appearance on Sleeping Cat's main street with her on his arm. He was touched by this and strangely angered; he'd not thought how the town might react, and he didn't care, really. Yet this was strange, for he'd always respected public opinion. He wondered if she would have trouble getting freed of her night's duties, and then he remembered a rumor that she was now part owner of the Bagdad. At first the talk had been that she was merely a hireling of Telford's. He thought again of the opulence of her room and was irked with himself because it seemed to matter.

He had the buggy out and was waiting upon the

seat when she appeared. She wore that cloak of navy blue she'd worn on the stagecoach, but as he helped her into the buggy, he saw that beneath the cloak she now wore a gingham dress. She said, "I hope I haven't kept you waiting."

He got her seated and drove out of Sleeping Cat; the basin night enfolded them, with only a few stars showing; and in this velvet darkness he headed north, skirting the eastern hills; and presently the road began climbing. The moon showed itself, lifting above the hills and spreading a day-bright luminosity over the basin. On a promontory he stopped the buggy and wheeled it around so that they were looking westward over the hill-cupped land.

At once he felt her stiffen and go away from him, even though she didn't move. He realized then what interpretation she'd put upon his stopping, and he was ashamed. He flung out an arm, taking in all the basin. "I've often stopped here for this view," he said. "There is none better in the lower hills. Have you ever seen such beauty?"

She said softly, "I suppose sometimes your wife rode with you."

"Yes," he said.

"I heard about your loss. I'm sorry."

He wheeled the buggy back into the ruts and drove onward, but now she'd put Sue into his thoughts, and he wondered if what he was doing tonight held some unfaithfulness to Sue. He had brought Cora along not for Mrs. Walker's need but for his own, a balm for loneliness, a man-need that was more than fleshly. He faced the truth of this, trying to be

honest, and knew only that a strange sort of joy
was his. He told himself that Sue would have understood.

When they came to Walker's hardscrabble spread,
lamplight stood in the window of a tar-papered shack;
and Luke Walker, hearing them coming, was outside and pacing his yard when Farrell stepped down
from the buggy. A stooped man, young-old and built
like a lodgepole pine, Walker showed a haggard face
in the moonlight.

"Is she having pain?" Farrell at once asked.

"No, but she's been fretting, afraid you wouldn't
get here in time." Walker clutched at Farrell's sleeve.
"Doc, you'll get her through this all right?"

"Certainly," Farrell said in his professional voice.
He handed Cora down. "This is Miss Dufrayne from
town, come out to help me."

If Walker recognized Cora from Sleeping Cat, he
gave no sign. He was a man near breaking from
worry; he ushered them into the tiny two-room shack,
blank with the blight of poverty; and Cora, at once
moving to the burlap partition that shut off the bedroom, vanished inside. Beyond that partition, Mrs.
Walker was moaning softly, monotonously. Farrell
set his kit upon the homemade kitchen table and
bustled about, moving to the stove to see that hot
water was ready, checking the contents of his kit.

Presently Cora reappeared. "I've got her dozing
now," she said. "Doctor, you look tired. I slept late
this morning. Why don't you try to rest? I'll call
you when the time comes."

"You might wait a minute too long."

She smiled. "Do you think I've never assisted at a birth? Now rest."

He thanked her with his eyes; he was indeed tired, and he seated himself by the table and urged Walker to sit, also. He began talking to the rancher. Afterward he could not remember that conversation; it was aimless, designed to keep Walker's mind from that next room. When at last sleep hung heavily on Farrell's eyelids, he admonished Walker to keep the fire going and the water hot; and then he permitted himself the luxury of sleep.

He was snatched from the woolly depths of slumber by Cora's voice, which now had a sharp note of insistence. He picked up his kit and made for the bedroom. At once he was all medico, brushing Luke Walker aside, working fast and efficiently; and always Cora was close by, responding to his demands, helping him.

Finally the moment came when she held a crying baby girl and the work was done; and Christopher Farrell straightened himself and looked across the bed and saw her, statuesque in the lamplight, the child in her arms. Out of this night there had come a kinship of work performed, and something more than that; and she made a picture now that impressed itself strongly upon him.

He said, "Thank you. Thank you so very much." And then he said, "I wish you could see yourself at this moment. You are the most beautiful sight in creation."

Now it was her turn to thank him, and she did, but only then did he see that she was silently weeping.

Chapter Eleven: HARD FISTS, HEAVY BOOTS

To CIRCLE-S THERE CAME A DAY when the gather was finished. Out of toil and sweat had come the building of the herd, the carrying to completion of the order, "Bring in everything that wears hair and horns." Thus on a certain summer morning, while the dew still stood on the grass and the meadow larks made bright music, the work went into a new phase, with Kittredge asking Dan Saxon to direct the cutting out of the cattle that would be delivered to railhead.

"You made the dicker," Kittredge said. "You do the choosing."

Saxon sat his saddle for a long, speculative moment, looking at the herd pridefully, for it was the proof of his skill as a cattleman. Careful breeding and planned grazing and strict attention to many details had gone into the making of the herd; one broken fence and one rampant bull from a lesser breed might have spelled ruination. Saxon looked, his aristocratic face showing sadness, the run of his thoughts plain to read. *This was mine, and this I lost.* Then he nodded at Kittredge and went about the work.

Through the herd Saxon rode, pointing out the prime beef, while men on cutting-horses criss-crossed the gather, skillfully chousing out the cows Saxon indicated. He selected the very best for this first delivery; a good showing would net Circle-S the contract to supply beef as long as the construction crews were in the hills. Such had been the intimation when the deal was made, and Saxon had told Kittredge about this.

All planning had been completed on the ranch-house gallery the night before, while the stars stood out and the coyotes mourned in the near-by hills and the bunkhouse threw lamplight on the hard-packed yard. A couple of men would stay behind when the trail drive started, their job being to let the rest of the herd graze over a wide area, yet keep them out of the hills so the whole roundup would not have to be repeated if the drovers came back from railhead with an immediate order for more beef. Also, these two would stand guard against any attack by Telford. Kittredge still expected such an attack and was fret-ful because he could not leave a stronger guard. Not and have enough men for the drive.

They argued as to whether the chuck wagon should come with the drive, Mather insisting that it would slow them on mountain terrain. But Saxon, who knew how morale would be lifted by a Dutch oven, was in favor of the chuck wagon. Kittredge thought about this as he watched the cutting and made a mental note to see the cook about supplies.

And so, through the day, the cutting went on, and they got the trail herd selected by late afternoon, a few hundred prime head. They decided to make the start early next morning. Kittredge was in favor of taking advantage of the remaining daylight, but Saxon shook his head. "We'll not be crossing the kind of country you find on the Texas llanos," he said. In all such matters Kittredge had made it his practice to defer to the judgment of Saxon and Mather, but when the morning came and they were at last ready to start, they learned of a difficulty they hadn't anticipated. The coosie, sour and forthright, told them.

"There ain't enough grub," he said. "What the hell was the notion of waitin' till the last minute to have me check?"

"But I got a wagonload from Barney Shay," Dan Saxon argued.

"And we've been eatin' off that for nearly two weeks," the cook reminded him. "By my calculations, it will take another week to get those cows to the railroad. We can't go that far on what's left. You want a chuck wagon on this drive, you better get somethin' to put inside it."

Saxon frowned. "Shay closed down the lid after that last load."

Kittredge, who'd heard all this, said, "That's my problem now." He turned to the coosie. "Make out a list of what you'll need—everything from Arbuckle's coffee on through the alphabet. The others can start pushing the herd along. Where's Pecos? He can head for town right now with a wagon. I'll follow him with the coosie's list and arrange for the grub."

Thus, while the herd was fashioned into the shape of a blunt arrowhead and pointed toward the higher hills, men at point and swing and some eating the dust of the drag, Reb Kittredge rode toward Sleeping Cat. Behind him he led the horse he'd rented from the livery stable. He set an easy, mile-eating pace; and far out on the basin's floor he wheeled his horse about and had a look toward the western hills. Like a faint banner, the lifted dust of the drive showed, and he was a sober man, deep-stirred by the sight.

He had worked roundups before, but this was *his* roundup, and the rush and roar of it had given him no time for such realization. Now he knew why Saxon had shown sadness at the gather's finish, and he felt charitable toward Saxon, remembering that the man had so far kept faith. Then he thought, *Hell, I'm getting soft!*

Facing about, he looked toward the distant buildings of Sleeping Cat and lifted his horse to a trot. Pecos, with the wagon, had an hour's start, and Kittredge was almost to town before he overtook the man. After that, he silently paced the wagon; and rider and rig came into Sleeping Cat together, Pecos pulling the wagon up before the mercantile store.

"Wait here," Kittredge told him and jangled his spurs inside.

The store was empty of customers, but Kittredge found George here and behind the counter, his other erstwhile companion at penny ante poker, Barney Shay. This bloodless man greeted him with a careful howdy holding no more warmth than a Vermont winter morning.

Kittredge laid the cook's list before Shay and said, "You can put this stuff in the wagon outside."

Shay pushed his steel-rimmed spectacles down on his nose, peered over them, cleared his throat twice, and said, "We run a strictly cash business."

Impatience touched Kittredge. "Rita Saxon came in here for cartridges not long ago. She got 'em."

"And she paid for them from her purse."

"She didn't tell me that," Kittredge said.

"Cash is our rule."

"In a cow town?" Kittredge asked wryly. "Do the ranchers hereabouts drive one cow to market every time they want to trade with you?"

"Sorry," Shay said, and became a fidgety man who obviously wished himself elsewhere.

"Okay," Kittredge said, "I've got the cash. It's in a Denver bank. Will you take an order on that bank?"

"Sorry; the rule is cash on the counter."

Kittredge stared at this man and understood then, for it was as though the dark shadow of Gault Telford lay across the pinched features of Barney Shay. Kittredge had expected an attack on Circle-S; and in the long night watches he had quickened to all alien sounds in the darkness, anticipating a raid. Twice during his nighthawking hitches he'd gone questing in the moonlight only to find he'd been made spooky by some vagrant shadow. There had been no raid because Telford had another way of closing out Circle-S, this shadowy way. He, Kittredge, had thought that Telford would strike with guns, but the Telfords shied from violence until no other way was left but violence. Telford had merely passed the word to Barney Shay, and Shay was now adamant. It was as simple as that.

Something stirred in Kittredge that edged his voice. "My men aren't going hungry because of your damn rule!" His own words sounded queer to him until he thought about them. *My men,* he'd said. That was the Circle-S bunch he'd bullied into submission by bullying Curly Mather, that bunch with whom he'd ridden and worked for only a couple of weeks. But the responsibility of feeding them had come also with the cut of the cards, and now he reached and got a grip on Barney Shay's shirt and drew the man halfway across his own counter. "Get at that loading!" Kittredge insisted.

"George!" Shay squawked.

The consumptive George had been making a great business of plying a broom in a far corner. He looked toward his employer; he looked as though he were about to burst into tears. He said, "I'm not bucking *him*."

Kittredge shook Shay until the man's spectacles bounced upon his nose and his teeth made a great rattling. "Now will you get at it?"

Shay's hands flailed at Kittredge; Shay's face turned red. "Let me go! You can have the grub!"

"Start loading it!" Kittredge snapped and released Shay.

Shay took the list and turned to the shelves and began piling canned goods upon the counter. Kittredge shouted at George, "Get over here and give him a hand," and George let the broom fall with a clatter and came running. Thereafter George carried load after load of merchandise out to the wagon. Kittredge, leaning against a cracker barrel, his arms folded and a wintry smile showing, merely watched, shaking his head when Pecos came in and made a move to help. "We're paying for the service, so we might as well have it," Kittredge told him.

Between them, Shay and George got the last item into the wagon. Kittredge waved a hand at Pecos. "Start rolling," he said.

Pecos gone, Kittredge said, "Fetch me pen and

ink. I'll draw up an order on that Denver bank."

He did this, then walked from the mercantile leaving a heavy silence behind him. He led the spare horse back to the livery stable and paid for its use from his pocket money. He came again to the street and stood on the edge of the boardwalk and rolled a cigarette. Presently he began to laugh. He was thinking, *I never even lifted my gun from leather;* and he was remembering George's frantic, "I'm not bucking *him*." Sometimes he hated being a legend, but today he'd laid his own dark shadow, and it had been greater than Telford's. He remembered why Curly Mather hadn't come to his feet fighting that day they'd tangled at Circle-S.

He finished his quirly and put his boot heel to it and was standing there contemplating the ugliness of Sleeping Cat when Dr. Farrell came along the street. Farrell stopped, showing Kittredge an uncompromising face, but his greeting was civil. He said, "I glimpsed you when you came riding in. I've been waiting a chance to speak to you."

"Well, you've got it," Kittredge said, amused at Farrell's crisp way. This was their first exchange of words since that day on the stagecoach, and he could see that Farrell still nourished a dislike for him. This raised its own antagonism in Kittredge. "What's on your mind?" he asked.

"At least one of the Jimsons is in town," Farrell said. "He's keeping under cover, but I caught a glimpse of him. If one of them is here, the other two are likely not far away."

"Then go tell the law," Kittredge said. "They tried

a holdup, didn't they?"

"The law," Farrell said stiffly, "is at the county seat, fifty miles from here. We've got a deputy sheriff, but he spends most of his time fishing."

Kittredge shrugged. "Then I guess you'll have to write him a letter."

Temper showed in Farrell's eyes and brought a red stain to his face. "Mr. Kittredge," he said, "I'm sorry you insist on being difficult. I feel that I owe you a turn for what you kept me from doing that day of the holdup. I'm trying to discharge that obligation. Are you so self-confident that a friendly warning is of no value? I'm remembering that the Jimsons threatened to kill you."

Kittredge saw now that some change had been wrought in Farrell. There was more self-assurance to the man and more charity. Kittredge said in a softer voice, "I'm sorry, Doc. And I'm grateful to you. I'll keep an eye peeled."

"Good day," Farrell said and went on up the street toward his cottage.

Whereupon Kittredge turned and began retracing his footsteps toward the mercantile where he'd left his own Circle-S horse. Farrell stayed in his mind; he saw him now as a proud man with his own particular code. He'd known no man exactly like Farrell, but he sensed that Farrell, though pliant, was not yet molded to the frontier. He remembered his own rough trails and wondered how the other would show himself in a truly tight situation. He remembered that wild play Farrell had contemplated during the holdup and shook his head. A jittery man when danger was in the air. His train of thought was broken by a small boy who came along the street and said, "Mr. Telford wants to see you."

Kittredge looked solemnly at the urchin. "Mr. Telford break a leg?"

"He's waiting in his office. He said he'd be pleased if you'd drop in."

Shay had likely run blubbering to his master, Kittredge reflected. But he crossed over in the direction the boy indicated and came to a small frame building set down upon the main street, a building so unpretentious that he'd paid it no heed that night he'd walked this street. He came through an open doorway into a dimly-lighted office, its air heavy with the piled-up heat of the day. In the semigloom he made out a squat iron safe, a few chairs, and a roll-top desk. In a creaking swivel chair before the desk sat Gault Telford, smiling benignly.

There were two other men in the room, silent men, truculent men, each standing with folded arms against a wall opposite from the other. Kittredge gave them his quick appraisal and his contempt; they were of the tumbleweed breed, hard-fisted and slow-thinking and for sale always at bargain prices. And now he knew the full value of Dr. Farrell's warning, for these were two of the Jimson brothers. One had a freshly healed wound on his hand where Kittredge had creased him the day of the holdup.

Kittredge said easily, "I thought you boys came in threes. Where's big brother?" He got only scowls for answer, and he said, "Which one of you did such a poor job of shooting at me the first night I was in town?"

One of them said, "That was Buck. He ain't here."

"Good," Kittredge said. "I'm glad one of you got a bellyful."

Telford spread his hands. "Sit down, Reb. They'll do you no harm unless you ask for it. They're merely here to protect me against you, if need be. All I want is five minutes of your time."

But Kittredge was wary. "I can manage to stand that long."

Telford's smile spread and seemed to encompass the room. "I've heard tell that you won Circle-S on the cut of a deck of cards."

Kittredge said, "Now, I didn't know that the news had got around."

"It isn't generally known. But the hotel clerk was at his desk that night. He was sleepy, but not too sleepy. He finds it wise to tell me things, and I find it wise to keep my little secrets. Is it true?"

"True."

"Have you got the papers? You know that a gambling-debt isn't legal and can't be collected in a Montana court of law, don't you?"

Kittredge hadn't known, but he said, "Isn't that my worry?"

"Yes, it is," Telford conceded. Again he made that spreading gesture with his hands. "I was merely trying to give you a friendly tip. Look, Reb, it's time this foolishness ended. I'll concede that you are the present owner of Circle-S. What is your price to sell to me and leave this part of the country?"

"I like ranching."

"You could stay and work as a ranch manager for me. I've made several such deals with former owners."

"You go to hell," Kittredge said.

Telford's eyes hardened behind those thick glasses. "That's your answer? Your final answer?"

"That's right."

Telford sighed; he looked like a man distressed by contemplating what he must do. He lifted his hand high, and Kittredge recognized the gesture as a signal. Kittredge had been watching the silent Jimsons, set like a pair of wooden cigar-store Indians. Too late, he anticipated the third one, the one who must have been posted where he could watch the doorway from cover. This one had now come close enough to respond to Telford's signal by stepping in through the open doorway behind Kittredge and wrapping an arm around Kittredge's throat, closing the arm sharply, elbow out.

Telford cried shrilly, "Get his gun! No, don't shoot, you fools! We can't have him murdered here in my office in broad daylight!"

Kittredge felt the gun plucked from his holster; he heard it clatter to the floor. He bent forward, trying to throw his assailant over his head. At once the other two came closing in; one slammed at Kittredge's jaw with a fist; another planted a heavy boot in his stomach.

He went down, writhing in pain and cursing himself for his cocksure carelessness. All three were upon him, striking and kicking. He fought back at them, knowing the futility of fighting against such odds but wanting to get in a few licks. He struggled to his feet, only to be borne down by the sheer weight of the three. Flame exploded in his brain, and blackness came after it; his last consciousness was of Telford leaning forward in his chair watching all this, an intent look on his face, an eagerness in his eyes.

Chapter Twelve: TO CIRCLE-S

KITTREDGE CAME FROM THE DARKNESS of oblivion to find himself in the darkness of night, the hard ground under him and the stars wheeling above, cold and remote. He lay in a half-world that made its harsh impression on him, yet lacked reality. His first awareness was of pain; pain was everywhere, running through all his muscles and clouding his thinking and making him wish for unconsciousness. Groaning, he closed his eyes again; but there was no escaping the pain.

Someone began tugging at his armpits, trying to get him to a stand. He fought feebly, not wanting to be moved, since it hurt to be moved. He cursed the man whose persistent hands kept at him; he wanted that man to go away.

Reality came back with a rush, and he remembered the trap into which he'd blundered and the beating he'd taken in Telford's office and knew then that he had been tossed into a back alley of Sleeping Cat like some common drunk. The Jimsons had certainly worked him over! He recalled Telford's sadistic pleasure; and anger obliterated pain, but only for a moment. Pain was a giant holding him tightly and warding off all else. He ceased fighting the man who was tugging at him; he had had enough of fighting.

"Dammit, you've got to get up on your laigs!" the man urged desperately. "Make a try now!" Kittredge recognized the voice; it was Pecos's.

Kittredge made the try, and with Pecos's help he got to a tottering stand. He had a hollowed-out feeling; he wasn't sure his legs would hold him. Yonder the sounds of Sleeping Cat rose to the sky—the beat of boots along the boardwalk, the wildness of the piano in the Bagdad, the lifted shout of a drunken cowpoke, the distant slamming of a door. Back here there were darkness and silence and pain.

The flame of anger still flickered, and Kittredge said, "Give me your gun!"

Pecos was a murky silhouette hovering near. "Your own's in your holster."

Kittredge felt and found it so, but the movement hurt. Odd that they would have left his gun on him. He began exploring himself for broken bones. Nausea moved through him in a compelling wave, and he tottered toward the rear of the nearest building, put his hand to its rough wall for support, and vomited. He stood for a moment, sick and weak and wretched, but his head was clearer. It struck him then that Pecos was supposed to be halfway across Sleeping Cat Basin with a load of grub. Damn it all, the crew needed that grub! He spoke of this hotly to Pecos.

"I got worried when you didn't come loping along after me," Pecos explained. "The fu'ther I got, the more worried I got. Finally I turned back. Nobody seemed to have seen you; nobody knew nothin' about you. Leastwise not the ones I talked to. But I found your horse tied up, so I knew you was still here. I kept lookin'."

"Where's the wagon now?"

Pecos grunted. "Edge of town."

"Let's get to it."

He was thinking with sudden panic that it would be too bad if Telford and the Jimsons found that wagon and removed the grub. He took a step and almost fell; queer how the ground seemed to buckle! Pecos was at once steadying him, and they moved along the alley with Kittredge lurching and staggering. At times his anger overrode his pain, and in such moments his thought was to go after Telford and his plug-uglies, yet common sense told him there had to be another day for that.

When they got to the outskirts of town, Kittredge perceived the outlines of the wagon and team. His own saddler had been hitched to the tailgate, but the horse looked twenty feet high.

"I'll ride in the wagon a piece," he said.

Pecos at once clambered into the wagon and began rearranging supplies. He was a hunched figure who worked hard for many minutes, while Kittredge leaned against a wagon wheel, fighting off sickness.

"Only got one blanket here," Pecos finally announced. "I've made room for you and spread it out. Climb in."

Kittredge set his boot to the wheel hub and reached with both hands for a grip on the wagon box and started pulling himself upward. Pain lanced the length of his right arm and spread through his body, and for a maddening moment he was sure he was going to faint. Pecos reached from the wagon and grasped at his shoulder, and Kittredge gritted his teeth and fought the pain. In this manner he was tumbled into the wagon like a sack of wheat. He fell upon the blanket, got to his hands and knees, and with a mighty effort managed to roll over and put his back to the blanket.

Pecos looked at him in the starlight, the oldster's lined face showing concern. He was a scared one, Pecos. "There's a sawbones in town," he said. "Fellow named Farrell. I'd best git you to him."

"No!" Kittredge said. "Get this wagon moving!"

"You wait a minute," Pecos said.

He hopped out of the wagon and started off toward town, and Kittredge called after him, "I don't want a doctor! Do you savvy? Don't bring Farrell!"

He didn't know whether Pecos heard him or would heed him, anyhow, and he cursed Pecos for a blundering fool. If Farrell came, all the tale might be told in Sleeping Cat before another sunset. And that tale mustn't be told, not the whole of it, anyway, not the fact that Reb Kittredge's gun arm had been beaten and stomped upon until it was nearly useless.

For that was the bitter truth he had to contemplate as he waited for Pecos. He had had one skill that set him above other men, one stock in trade; and it had made him a legend, the kind of legend that Curly Mather had been afraid to buck hard, the kind of legend that had scared Barney Shay and George into loading this wagon with grub. But the Jimson brothers, with their angry fists and boots, had made him a shorn Samson. The restoring of his gun to its holster, he now realized, had been the last ironic touch before they'd heaved him into an alley. And now he could only lie here and curse them till his breath was spent, curse them and hope that Farrell wouldn't come to gauge the real extent of the damages. He couldn't count on Farrell as a friend; Farrell had already discharged the only debt he felt he owed Reb Kittredge.

At least no bones had been broken, Kittredge reflected savagely. But his muscles had been pounded and stomped until the resilience was gone from them. He supposed that time would heal him, but he wondered how long it would take. A week? Two weeks? Longer? He grew fretful and worried over what was keeping Pecos. He felt of his forehead and found it hot. And then he heard Pecos returning.

The old-timer climbed into the wagon box and silently handed over a pint of whisky. Kittredge got the bottle to his lips with an effort and put his teeth to the cork. He let the whisky run freely; it spread fiery fingers through him; it warmed his stomach and numbed the pain, and the world was less dark than it had been.

Pecos peered at him in the starlight. "How many of 'em was there?"

"Three. The Jimson brothers. Telford was there, too, damn him. He watched."

"They didn't mark your face much."

Kittredge managed a wry grin. "It wasn't my good looks they were trying to spoil."

Pecos shook his head. "No, I reckon it wouldn't be that."

Again the whole horrible realization of his impotency rose to smite Kittredge, and fear put an edge to anger. Once he had seen a hamstrung horse; now he knew how it felt to be so helpless. He tried to raise his right arm, but pain gave him a sharp reminder of its uselessness, so he raised his left instead. He got his hand on Pecos's shirt front, and he said, "Circle-S isn't to know about this—not all of it, anyway! Do you understand? I got in a saloon fight and got roughed up a little. Something like that. But you're telling no one that I couldn't lift myself into this wagon! Is that clear?"

Pecos had an edge of righteous anger to his voice. "Now who the hell would I be telling?"

Kittredge let go of the man. "I'm sorry. You'd better get this wagon moving."

"Sure," Pecos said. "Those boys'll be a mite hungry by the time we catch up to 'em."

Kittredge said, "You're a good man, Pecos."

Pecos grunted, clambered to the wagon seat, and shook out the reins, and the wagon began moving westward. At once it was a jolting rack, making a bed of torture for Kittredge. He moved himself about, as far as the limited space permitted, trying to find a more comfortable position. He closed his eyes and set his teeth against the pain.

He was to remember that ride always, himself flat on his back, with the stars blurring above him and the constant *clop-clop* of the horses' hoofs in his ears. He would have sworn that the wagon had square wheels. At times he was certain he would find it less painful aboard the saddler, and he was of a mind to ask Pecos to stop the wagon and help him mount the trailing horse. At times he fainted, and these were the blessed moments, bringing him oblivion. He nipped at the whisky bottle sparingly, but he had drained it long before they reached Circle-S's acreage.

He supposed that fever overcame him, for he had moments of wild imaginings; and his mind shuttled to forgotten yesterdays, bringing these back in mismated shards of memory. One moment he was a boy in Texas fashioning his first *reata;* the picture of that stood out with startling clarity only to blend with that day at the T-A ranch a decade later when Colonel Van Horn swung his cavalry between the ranch house and the besieging force under Arapahoe Brown and brought to an end the Johnson County war. Thus he whisked through time and space.

He thought again of that blacksmith toiling at his forge late of a night in a town he'd not been able to remember when he'd watched another blacksmith his first night in Sleeping Cat. It struck him suddenly that the town had been Denison on the Red River, and he was jubilant with the remembrance. He wanted to tell someone, but it came to him that nobody else cared.

The hours were endless hours; the miles were endless miles. By tipping his head far back, he could see Pecos upon the seat; but even such effort cost him pain. A time or two Pecos had to stop and dismount and open gates, and Kittredge blessed these moments when the jolting ceased, and he wished that the wagon had never to move again. But always it did.

When they finally came into Circle-S's yard and

Pecos announced their whereabouts, Kittredge was surprised; for he'd lost all sense of time and distance. Also, he was fretful. He said weakly, "We've got to catch up with that trail herd."

"Not tonight," Pecos said. "We've got to get us some sleep. And a change of horses."

Getting out of the wagon was even more difficult than climbing in had been. The yard was formless, dark as the inside of a boot; and Kittredge, realizing that this was the darkness before dawn, knew that Pecos had chosen a slow and careful route homeward. He was mighty grateful to Pecos and tried saying so, but talking required too much effort, and his voice trailed away. He felt Pecos's arm about him and let the old-timer guide him across the yard. That traverse seemed to take forever. At the gallery steps, Kittredge stumbled. Pecos got him up the steps and into the house and to Dan Saxon's bedroom.

Here Kittredge must have fainted again, for his next consciousness was of being in bed, and he discovered that he'd been stripped naked. The bed felt good to him, so pleasurable as to be almost an agony. He burrowed deep into the bed and let its softness cradle him.

Presently he heard movement in the house. He listened and judged that Pecos must be somewhere about. He heard voices and listened even harder, wondering who was here with Pecos. He guessed that one of the hands who'd been left with the gathered herd had come to the ranch. This made him fretful again; suppose Telford were to top one coup with another by attacking this very night? He tried to identify that cowpoke's voice; they had become individuals to him this past week, those Circle-S men.

At the moment he realized it was not a man speaking, Rita came into the bedroom. He couldn't understand this; Rita had gone with the trail herd and should be ten or fifteen miles along the way. But she was here. She came to the bedside and stood, an indistinct shape in the darkness, someone he sensed more than saw.

"Where are you hurt?" she asked.

"All over," he said, his voice thick. "My arms and chest mostly."

She seated herself on the edge of the bed and ran her hands under the blankets, and he felt her fingers upon his aching flesh, soft and soothing. She began to manipulate the muscles of his shoulders and arms, her manner as cool and impersonal as a medico's. Her fingers moved constantly, not probing too hard when his wincing indicated she had touched an especially sore spot. She worked for many minutes; her fingers had a magic in them that smoothed the sharper edges of pain away and brought him a pleasant lassitude.

He asked sleepily, "Where did you learn to do this?"

"From a Mexican woman who was my nursemaid when I was a child. My mother's people were Spanish, you know. From Chihuahua. My mother and father met in Texas; and when my father trailed north, Doña Theresa came along. Her family had served my mother's family for generations. She knew many such tricks as this one, that old Doña Theresa. Often she eased the soreness of *vaqueros* who'd been pitched from horses. She also had a way with knife and bullet wounds."

Her voice was soft in the darkness, gentle as her fingers; and he knew that her languid talk was part of the ministrations, meant to soothe him. He asked, "Your mother? She passed away?"

Her voice caught. "On that drive north. We met Comanches in the Nations who demanded tribute to let us pass through their territory. Thirty horses they wanted. My father knew he'd need those horses in Montana, so he refused, and there was a fight. My mother was killed by a Comanche arrow. She is buried on the bank of the Canadian."

"Then you couldn't have known her."

"Not ever. But sometimes when my father talks about her, I feel that I know her."

He said, "I'm sorry."

He surrendered himself to the magic of her fingers and was conscious of her nearness and comforted by it. At last his eyes grew heavy, and he was wafted outward to the sweet forgetfulness of sleep.

Chapter Thirteen: THE HIGH ROAD

HE AWOKE TO A ROOM WARM AND GOLDEN with sunlight and was content to lie in Dan Saxon's bed and enjoy such languid luxury. He had slept well, and he was strangely at peace with himself until remembrance came rushing; and he thought of many things then, of Gault Telford's play and Pecos's loyalty and the discovery of his own uselessness when he'd tried to clamber into the wagon. Also, he thought of that trail herd climbing into the hills, all the hopes of Circle-S riding with it; and he bestirred himself, tossed aside the blankets, and got from the bed.

He was sore in every muscle, but not as sore as he'd supposed he would be. He remembered Rita's soothing fingers; but that was like a dream remembered, pleasant to contemplate but without reality. He tried walking and found that his legs obeyed him; the world had regained its old stability. He saw that his clothes were here in the room, tossed carelessly aside when Pecos had stripped him. He got into them, being slow about this.

When he'd latched his gun belt about his waist, he tried a few practice draws. His right arm now moved to his will without sharp pain clamoring through him; but the movement was sluggish, lacking that extra edge of speed that made all the difference. He would have to favor that arm for a long time. His thinking grew somber then; he had lost the sense of peace with which he had awakened. He remembered the fists and boots of the Jimsons and knew that he had been spared from death only because Telford hadn't wanted murder done publicly. The Telfords were the careful ones, keeping a wary eye on the law they always managed to flout. But now Reb Kittredge had been readied for the kill; the Jimsons would only have to wait their chance.

So thinking, Kittredge went out upon the gallery and looked upon the golden morning and at once saw that Pecos's wagon was gone. The ranch had an emptiness, the serenity of desertion. He lifted his eyes to the hills and thought of the crew up there, and Pecos hard on their trail. He felt suddenly lonesome, and this for him was a strange feeling; for he had long walked alone, not caring. He saw that smoke lifted from the cookshack chimney; and as he looked that way, Rita framed herself in the shack's doorway and beckoned. Lifting his hand to her, he crossed the yard.

"Breakfast is ready," she said.

Nodding, he recalled that he'd not eaten since yesterday. He washed himself at the basin on the bench, ran a hand over the stubble on his chin, and came inside and took a chair. "Pecos got started early?" he asked.

"He thought the grub should get delivered."

He began eating; she served him in that same cool, impersonal manner she'd displayed last night. He watched her move from stove to table and back again; he saw the easy grace of her and remembered Dan Saxon's agile hands and knew from whom she'd inherited her quickness. He said, "Thanks for what you did last night."

She turned her back and busied herself with the coffeepot. "How do you feel?"

"Able to ride."

She refilled his coffee cup and went outside. When he'd finished eating and had his cigarette, he walked over to the corrals and found that she'd saddled two horses. He took up the reins of one and made ready to mount; and then, remembering, he shifted the reins from his left hand to his right, grasped the horn with his left hand, and hauled himself up, making an awkward mount. His back was to Rita, and he wasn't sure whether she saw how he'd handled himself, but at least she said nothing. They lined out together and rode from the yard.

"This way," she directed.

The spoor of the trail herd was easy to follow; and they moved along the base of the hills in the morning's brightness, riding stirrup to stirrup for the first few miles. Then they began climbing an old logging road that rose in gentle pitches into the timber and took a tortuous way.

Kittredge, who'd worked cattle on the open Texas plains, whistled to himself. Here the herd must have been forced down till the cows moved four or five abreast, but at least the palisade of pine on either side of the road had done the work of the flanking riders. He wondered how much time the drive had made on such terrain. Ten miles the first day, he judged. It was now nearly high noon, and he estimated that it would be deep dark before they would come upon the herd. He kept looking ahead for Pecos's wagon; but since they didn't overtake it, he decided that Pecos had indeed got an early start.

The saddle was punishment, but he tried not to show it. Remembering the wagon's jolting of the night before, he was surprised that the saddle hurt him no more than it did; and again he remembered Rita's fingers. There must have been ancient magic in her ministrations, something handed down from the primitive ones; and he blessed the name of Doña Theresa. Later on, when Rita pointed out a short cut and they left the logging road to follow a narrow game trail across the broken face of the hillside, he contrived to ride behind her and took secretly to massaging his right arm.

This game trail led them back to the logging road in due course; and in midafternoon they came upon a grassy mountain meadow, cupped high on the hillside. Here serviceberry bushes showed and wild raspberry, and Indian paintbrush lifted above the grass. And here the drovers had made camp the night before. In the center of the meadow the sign was plain to read—the black scar where the coosie's fire had been built, the trampled grass where the herd had bedded, the droppings of the *remuda*. Kittredge found the very spot where the chuck wagon had stood and detected the fresh signs of the passage of Pecos's wagon.

"Well, we made better time than the herd did," he observed.

Rita raised her hand, pointing up the hillside. "Up there," she said.

Kittredge listened intently, standing in his stirrups and leaning forward. Across the bright-blue sky a hawk wheeled; in the brush a magpie chattered. Somewhere near by a mountain creek splashed over rocks and made raucous music. Yet in this high, still air Kittredge thought he detected remote sounds of men and movement, distant and illusive, the faint bawling of cattle, the popping of rope ends, the lifted voices of the drovers. Or was that some fantasy born of expectation? He wasn't sure, and presently he gave up listening, and they began riding again.

Darkness overtook them all too soon. There was a

brief twilight after the sun had plunged behind the hills, a time when all the world hushed down; and then the trail became a black tunnel. The night world came to life; claws rattled on rock, and a questing owl slid overhead, and somewhere far away a coyote mourned. As the riders felt their way along, the timber thinned, and the basin lay like a lake of darkness below them, broken by the scattered pin points of light that marked the ranches, and the distant twinkling cluster that was Sleeping Cat. The air grew colder.

Now Kittredge had to trust to Rita's judgment, but she knew the country well and led the way in a silence that was broken only by her occasional warnings of low-hanging branches or abrupt turns of the trail. They moved onward and upward, and presently the moon lifted over the far hills to the east, though little of its light filtered down through the tangle of treetops that again made a canopy.

Shortly thereafter, Kittredge heard the bawling of cattle. He tried to orient the sound, but it was a vagrant ghost roaming the night. But the sound grew louder, drawing them; and after an hour they burst upon another of those mountain meadows and saw a campfire burning ahead. Shortly they rode into the circle of its light.

Here stood the high tilts of the chuck wagon, and Pecos's wagon was near by. Yonder, the bedded herd made a dark blur upon the slope; and within the firelight's rim stood Dan Saxon, a two-day's beard stubble showing on his aristocratic face and his hand no longer bandaged—Dan Saxon, and the grizzled

Pecos, and a few of the Circle-S hands who were not otherwise employed. And Curly Mather. Their faces were turned toward the disturbed darkness; they held an expectancy for either friend or foe.

Pecos said with a gusty sigh, "It's them," and the tautness left all the group save one.

As Rita stepped down from her saddle, Mather said, "I see you found him."

His tone held a truculence which revealed both anger and jealousy; and Kittredge came at once to the ground and stood ready, sensing that Mather's imaginings had pressed him to the exploding-point. He felt sorry for Mather in this moment, sorry that any man should be so prodded as to make such a display of himself. Yet he also felt the full force of Mather's hatred. There'd have to be a showdown be-between him and Mather some day. That had been inevitable from the moment in Circle-S's yard when he had felled Mather, and from just such a spark as this could come the explosion.

Rita said, "I'm tired, Curly, and hungry. Whatever you've got to say can keep till later."

"No!" Mather snapped and took a quick step toward her, seizing her arm. "You've made a fool of me, running off to see what was keeping him."

Rita cried, "Let go!" and wrenched free of Mather.

Dan Saxon's face hardened, and he took one belligerent step toward Mather.

Kittredge said, his voice like a whiplash, "That's enough, Curly!"

He faced Mather, remembering then that he could not stand up against Mather with either fist or gun, not since last night. He felt tension build within the firelight's rim. A couple of the crew who'd been working, one at mending a bridle, another at limbering up a stiff rope, let their work drop. The looseness went out of Pecos; and in the heavy silence the popping of a stick in the fire was like an explosion. There was a drawn-out moment when Kittredge and Mather stood with eyes locked, flint and stone striking sparks. For the space of a watch tick, Kittredge was sure Mather would come at him. The wild intent was naked on his face. Then Mather dropped his eyes and, turning, strode off into the darkness.

Kittredge shrugged. "Where's the coosie?" he demanded. "I'm hungry."

But he was thinking, *Sooner or later he'll find out I've been cut into the culls!* He felt Pecos's eyes on him; he remembered that Pecos shared his secret. Pecos was the one who knew how near death Reb Kittredge had just stood.

"Here's grub," the cook called from the shadows by the chuck wagon.

Kittredge got a plate for himself and one for Rita. He ate his supper, seated cross-legged on the ground, and dropped the plate in the wrecking-pan. He smoked a cigarette in silence, aware that the men around the fire were also silent. He supposed that Pecos had spun them some windy about what had happened in town, and they were now probably waiting for his own version. But when he'd stomped out his quirly, he rolled into a blanket on the ground.

The fire died, and the others bedded down. He found Rita's tarp next to his own, and after an hour she came to him silently; he felt her fingers probing at him, working last night's magic, that ancient art that had been born in Mexico and come from there to Texas and thence to Montana. Again he was soothed to sleep, grinning wryly with the thought that Curly Mather ought to see them now!

In the morning there was all the confusion of getting the trail herd under way, but before full daylight they were wending onward, Mather riding in point position and the chuck wagon jolting far ahead. There was a day of this, and another and another; and one of those days they made only five miles, for the country grew wilder and more rugged, and sometimes the trail was a mere thread through the wilderness, and sometimes there was no trail at all.

To Kittredge, the drive was a revelation. He'd seen cattle moved but never over this kind of country. The hours became a fantasy of constant timber and winding trail, and sometimes there were deadfall logs to be snaked aside by saddle ropes, and sometimes the chuck-wagon ax was put to use to clear the way. They lost cattle; a few broke legs, and the crippled beasts had to be shot. Pecos's wagon was abandoned once the grub had been transferred to the chuck wagon, and even that piece of equipment became such a mixed blessing that Saxon conceded his mistake in bringing it along. There was talk of sending back to Circle-S for pack horses and abandoning the chuck wagon, too; but with the drive now so high in the hills, they decided against this. And so they pushed onward, a grim, relentless cavalcade, the steady bawling of the cattle lifting in the thin air.

Each night they bedded the herd and guarded it through the long watches, but no longer was there room to ride circle. By day they fought the mountain's pitch and the mountain's many faces. Always Mather kept apart from Kittredge now, speaking only when he needed to, and always Kittredge watched himself, not wanting to betray to any of them that he'd returned less than a whole man. The effects of his beating were wearing off with the passing days, but still the saddle punished him; and when he tried his gun arm in his secret moments, he found improvement in his speed but was far from satisfied. This fretted him and made him morose.

Then, on the third day after Kittredge had rejoined the herd, Dan Saxon lifted his hand in the stillness of the afternoon; and when the others strained their ears at this signal, they also heard what Saxon had heard, the distant, mournful hoot of a locomotive in these high reaches, the clanging of the locomotive's bell. Thereafter, Saxon rode on ahead of the herd; and when the night camp was made, he returned jubilant.

"The rails have been moving, too," he reported. "The construction camp is a good deal nearer than it was when I first made the dicker. We'll have this beef delivered by tomorrow afternoon."

The men were a beaten bunch, worn thin by the arduous uphill trail; but they stirred to life at the news and even raised a ragged cheer. The cook spread a treat for supper, a row of dried-apple pies, each with Circle-S's brand cut into the crust. Kittredge looked about him at the drawn, bearded faces; and sharing both their tiredness and their jubilation, he was one with his crew.

Afterward Rita wandered off afoot in the darkness. Kittredge saw her go, and on impulse he moved after her. She had found a trail that wove through the timber, and he followed along this trail until it came upon a high, rocky ledge that overlooked the basin. Now the lights of Sleeping Cat were far more remote than they'd been that first night he and Rita had climbed the high road. Rita stood here in the starlight, her back to him; she stood looking upon the panorama below. He came behind her and said softly, "Rita?"

"Yes?" she said, not turning.

He'd had little communication with her since they'd joined the drive. He'd followed her tonight with no intent he could have named, but now he slipped his arms around her. She turned within the circle of his arms and faced him. He looked at her in the starlight and saw her sultry sadness; he looked at those full lips so rich in promise. He smiled then, knowing why he'd come.

He said softly, "Do you know, that first night I thought you'd decided to stay at the ranch instead of going along with the drive. I didn't understand until Curly spoke up that you'd turned back to find me."

She looked away from him. "The grub was important to the drive. We all began to worry when you and Pecos didn't join us on the trail."

She was keeping her voice even, and he knew she was trying to imply that it hadn't been for him she'd turned back. But he also knew her calm was costing her effort. And he was conscious of her suppleness within his arms, conscious that she wasn't moving away from him. He tightened his arms around her and drew her close, and his lips went seeking hers. For a moment she fought against him, turning her face aside, and then her lips were on his. Her arms closed about him and her fingers strayed to the nape of his neck. For a long moment they were thus, and then she was pushing him away.

"No!" she cried.

"Rita! Rita!" he murmured, not understanding.

"Tomorrow it's all over. This isn't just a way for me to stay on Circle-S. And that's what you'd come to think some day."

He put his hands to her shoulders and held her at arm's length. "You're wrong. You're very wrong."

Beyond her, he could see Sleeping Cat so far below, so far away. Down there were Gault Telford and the Jimsons and Cora Dufrayne and Dr. Farrell; and he thought of them fleetingly, and of Dan Saxon and Pecos and Curly Mather, too. None of them had been known to him until a short while ago, and now all of their lives were caught up with his in the same web. But tomorrow would come victory for him, and this was what he wanted to share, and Rita was the one he wanted to share it with. The lives of the others had made their impact on his, but Rita had come to matter more than all the rest. He knew this now in the night and the silence, and it held a glory beyond any previous knowledge.

But she was saying, "No, Reb. No."

Then he heard the faint stirring in the timber behind him, and the alarm on her face told him she'd heard, too. He wheeled about, placing himself between her and whatever moved in the brush; and he got his gun out and stood with it in his hand, keening the darkness. He heard the sound again, fainter this time. He called, "Who's there?"

There was only silence; no answer came back but the empty echo of his voice.

Chapter Fourteen: CATASTROPHE

THEY MADE READY TO MOVE THE HERD in the darkness before dawn. Mountain chill hung heavily on the camp, and the cook-fire showed bright against the black face of the hill. Men moved sluggishly about their business, and Dan Saxon came to Kittredge in the midst of the confusion.

"Curly's gone," Saxon reported.

Kittredge had just taken the early morning kinks out of his horse in a hard pitching session. He dismounted after the fashion of a roper, leaping from his saddle so that he wouldn't have to lower himself by the use of his arm. He moved close to Saxon. "Yes?" he asked.

"I didn't miss him last night," Saxon said. "But I've asked a few questions this morning. Curly took a walk right after supper. He came back shortly, looking as black as any thundercloud, so the boys tell me. He rolled up his blankets, cut his private saddler out of the *remuda*, and rode off without even a so-long."

Kittredge fashioned up a cigarette, his mind harking back to the night before; and he knew now who'd made movement in the brush when he'd been holding Rita in his arms on the rocky ledge yonder. Mather had followed them and spied upon them, and then Mather had quit the drive. Kittredge and Rita had come back to the camp at once and gone directly to their soogans, and it had been Kittredge's judgment at the time that some animal had prowled the brush. Now he knew differently. He turned the knowledge over in his mind and was sorry for Curly Mather. The man had had his own kind of strength and savvy, but it hadn't been enough.

"He's got some pay due him," Kittredge said.

"I'll know where to find him when the time comes," Saxon said and turned away.

In the first flush of dawn, Kittredge watched him go. Saxon hadn't shaved since leaving the ranch; and his beard, gray-shot and inclined to curl, gave him an added dignity. Moreover, it hid his mouth and made him a harder man to read than before. He'd given his report on Mather with no more concern than if he'd mentioned a limping horse or some other small nuisance of the day. Yet the feeling was in Kittredge that Saxon had foreseen Mather's desertion. It was as though all men were to Saxon the cards in a deck, as though Saxon, the gambler always, had judged Mather's worth and had expected what would show when the deck was shuffled. Once Kittredge had had the feeling that Dan Saxon was unbeatable. How could you jar a man who always knew how the cards would fall?

Thinking this, Kittredge remembered Telford's

claim—that a gambling-debt couldn't be legally collected. Yet Saxon had been ready to remove himself from Circle-S the morning Kittredge had ridden out to take over. Had that been a bluff on Saxon's part, a move in a carefully calculated game? Come to reflect on it, Saxon might even be playing *him* like a card! But he believed not.

To the east, dawn's riotous colors stood over the distant hills, and grayness filtered into the woods where the camp stirred. Rope ends were popping, and riders made movement in the chilly murk. Pecos came past Kittredge and showed him a sour face. Pecos said, "Now what the hell did I do with last summer's pay?" Already the chuck wagon was lumbering ahead, and the herd was being shaped up and pointed on its way.

Shrugging, Kittredge put out his quirly, rose to saddle, and went to work. A man made his choices; Curly Mather had made his. But Kittredge was remembering Rita pushing him, Kittredge, away last night and crying, "Tomorrow it's all over." Mather had wanted to marry Rita, and Mather's chance had been the strong chance, but he hadn't waited to learn that. With a cut of the cards, Reb Kittredge had won everything—save Rita! Now why hadn't Mather savvied that?

They began moving the herd along, and the morning came strong and clear, sunlight dispelling the chill of the high-country dawn. The cattle were strung out through the pines, men toiling to keep them in line; they moved across the face of the hill; they moved toward the sky. Kittredge looked for

Rita and saw her riding in swing position; sometimes she was lost to sight as she darted here and
there at her work. Kittredge was at drag, with bunch-
quitters to keep him busy.

He thought he recognized that old mossy-horn that
had charged him his first day in the saddle for
Circle-S. He laid the end of his rope across the mossy-
horn's rump. "How the devil did you get cut into
the prime beef?" he demanded.

He looked for Rita whenever he was free enough
to do so. He hoped she'd ride back and join him, but
she kept her distance, and he knew that she wished it
that way. Once she'd spoken to him of pride, and now
he knew how strong hers was. He was remembering
her saying, "This isn't just a way for me to stay on
Circle-S. And that's what you'd come to think some
day." He was remembering her pushing him away.

He had been a selfish man, keeping his eyes always
on his own ambition, riding roughshod over all the
land. From the first, he'd supposed that Rita was as
selfish. Now he thought about last night, the wonder
of it, and the bitterness, and was perplexed and a
little angry; for he'd come up against something beyond his experience and understanding. He felt as
he had that day when he'd dug the arrowhead from
the Circle-S shutter and flung it angrily away, not
knowing why he'd done it.

The mournful wail of a locomotive drifted over
the hills again, the sound seeming to be almost in
their midst. The cattle showed spookiness, and every
rider was at once sweating to keep them in line. This
would be a hell of a place for a stampede, Kittredge

reflected. Presently he made out the chuffing of a work train, the beat of hammers against spikes, the clanging of rails being lowered into place. Men's voices reached him in tattered, meaningless fragments. These sounds haunted the mountain air. The Circle-S crew quickened and began giving stricter attention to their work, but the men took to smiling.

Just past noon they broke out of timber, and in the openness before them they saw their destination. Across the shoulder of the hill ran the yellow welt of the grade, loose ties strewn aimlessly beside it. Teamsters were shouting at work horses; this sound blended with the clanging sledges and the hissing of steam from a locomotive. Weather-beaten tents and construction shacks were scattered upon the flat, an ugly makeshift town. Men were everywhere, swarming about like ants. And the Circle-S herd, spilling from the pines, advanced upon them, advanced upon end-of-steel.

The chuck wagon up front did not stop for the preparation of a noonday meal. Circle-S would eat at tables in the commissary shack today. They drove on, their hunger forgotten, their weariness sloughed away; and shortly Dan Saxon, riding point position, made the circling movement of his hand that signaled for the herd to be milled and bedded.

While this was being done, Saxon spurred back to Kittredge. "Well," Saxon said, crow's-feet of laughter pulling at the corners of his eyes, "we've delivered a beef herd."

"Let's get it finished," Kittredge said.

Saxon bawled orders to the crew; then he and

Kittredge rode into the construction camp. They were looking for the grading contractor who would buy the beef; and at last they found him in a crude shack where a telegraph instrument clattered, a stoop-shouldered operator hunched over it. The contractor was a big man with a hearty voice, and he gave his hand to Saxon and was introduced to Kittredge.

"One of my foremen has already looked over the beef and reported to me," the contractor told Saxon. "It's fine-looking stuff."

Saxon said, "You can hand over the payment to Mr. Kittredge. And you can talk to him about future deliveries. He's the new owner of Circle-S."

The contractor frowned. "There's a hitch."

"A hitch?"

The contractor tipped his head toward the telegraph instrument. "A wire came this morning from the sheriff at the county seat. He ordered the cash impounded that I was to have paid you for the beef. The money is to go to a Mr. Gault Telford of Sleeping Cat to meet notes he holds against Circle-S. Notes now overdue."

Dan Saxon said very quietly, "Those notes are not due for another sixty days."

The contractor waved an arm. "That's something you'll have to settle with this fellow Telford. I can't be involved in personal squabbles. Neither can I go bucking local law, if I want to get this spur finished. I'll take the beef if you're willing to leave it. I've got hungry men to feed. But you'll have to straighten out that matter of the money before I can turn it over to you."

Kittredge said, "Keep the beef."

He turned then and walked from the shack. It came to him that he was very tired and that the work of the fists of Telford's plug-uglies was still taking its toll. He walked along blindly in the strong sunlight; he walked through all the chaos of the construction camp with no conscious thought. Men brushed by him, sometimes shouldering him out of the way. Once the wheel of a freight wagon narrowly missed him, and he was roundly cursed by the teamster for his carelessness. He gave the teamster an unsmiling stare, not really hearing the man.

He walked until he came to a frame-and-canvas structure that bore the crude legend: *Saloon*. He stared at the makeshift sign until its meaning penetrated his consciousness, and then he turned inside and found a sawdust-strewn floor and a plank bar. Silence and coolness were here, and only the bartender was present at this hour. From him Kittredge ordered whisky. He downed the drink fast and felt it warm him, and he ordered again but left the second drink untouched for a long time. He stared into its amber depths, then toyed with the glass, making little patterns on the planking.

Catastrophe had numbed him. All his thinking was wooden, and at the core of it was a gnawing hatred for Gault Telford. Overdue notes! A flick of the pen would have changed the dates, and Telford himself would probably have that sort of skill. Telford had planned this little sandy from the first, timing it so the sheriff would have his piece spoken over the railroad telegraph before the beef got to the camp.

Kittredge downed his drink and crooked a finger at the bartender.

Once he, Kittredge, had expected a raid on Circle-S and he'd stood alert and ready for that raid. Then he'd supposed that Telford had satisfied himself with the beating that the Jimsons had inflicted. But the Telfords played a different kind of game, and the beating had only been part of it. The beating was to have kept Reb Kittredge from retaliating when the real play was made, retaliating with a fast gun. Kittredge made a pistonlike motion with his right arm. Pretty stiff yet.

He found another drink before him. He dug out all his pocket silver and spread it on the bar, letting it lie. He saw the bartender's hand slide forward and extract a coin from the pile. A fat, pudgy hand. Not the quick, graceful kind of hand Dan Saxon had. One more like Gault Telford's.

"Belly-crawling snake," Kittredge said.

He was hungry, he realized, and he thought to find the crew and join them at table. He owed the crew wages, he recalled; he was a ranch owner now. Well, there was enough money left in that Denver bank to take care of them. He began to laugh, thinking how he'd finished out a circle. He would go back to Texas busted flat, back to being another forty-a-month cowpoke, a little older and a hell of a lot wiser.

"Easy come, easy go," he said aloud.

The bartender said sympathetically, "You look like a man with things on your mind, friend."

"Yes," Kittredge said slowly, "you're right on the

first guess, my fat friend. I am thinking about killing a man. I am thinking about killing him because there is no other way his kind can be stopped. How do you outsmart a spider? You don't. You tear his web from its dusty corner and stomp the whole business, spider and all, under your heel. That's the way you fix a spider. Isn't it so?"

The bartender looked startled, his flabby mouth sagging. Then he said soothingly, "Have one on the house. No use being in a hurry about that killing. It can wait until tomorrow."

Kittredge took the drink that was slid across the bar. "Sure, it can wait."

He bought a drink for himself and one for the bartender. He decided that the bartender was a very understanding man, a good fellow to be with when the maggots were crawling in your brain and you faced your own defeat and didn't like the looks of it. He had still another drink. Come to think of it, what sense was there in killing Telford? They only put a rope around your neck for that kind of cavorting, so in the end you were just as dead as Telford. No, he'd been licked, and he might just as well tuck his tail between his legs and skulk back to Texas and start over again.

"Tomorrow it's all over," Rita had said. How right she'd been!

"You're laughing," the barkeep said. "It's good for a man to laugh. Drink up!"

Kittredge fixed his gaze on the man. "Think hard now," Kittredge said thickly. "Who's the biggest damn fool that ever came in this place?"

The bartender said, "Well, mister—"

Kittredge shook his head. "It's no use. You name the biggest damn fool of them all, and he's still a second-rater compared to me." He looked down and found his glass empty. He said testily, "How long does a man have to wait for a drink in this shebang?"

The bartender was staring toward the door, surprise on his flabby face. Kittredge heard Rita then. She was crying, "Reb!"

He turned very slowly, keeping one elbow on the bar because he liked the solid feel of it. He saw her in the doorway of the saloon, and his muddled thought was that this was a hell of a place for her to be.

She came toward him and said, "I've been looking all over for you!"

"And now you've found me," he said.

Her face was taut with agitation, but he was thinking that she was the loveliest thing he'd ever known. She was softness and sturdiness, fire and ice; she was all of a man's dreaming.

"It's Dad," she said. "He's gone!"

"He's down at the telegraph shack." He laughed. "He's talking big business."

"No, he left there more than an hour ago. They tell me he took a fresh horse and headed out." Her hand closed on his arm, that useless right arm; he felt the hard pressure of her fingers. "Reb, I think he's gone looking for Gault Telford. I talked to the contractor. Dad told him he intended to make Telford admit those notes were doctored."

He was nearly sober then; it was as though cold

water had been flung on him. His mind was a great fuzziness, but he could grasp one fact and cling to it. He said, "That's my job! If anybody braces Telford, it's going to be me!"

She said, "But your gun arm's no good. Don't you think I saw how you mounted your horse that first day? And I've watched you being careful since and rubbing your arm when you thought no one was looking. You're in no shape for fighting!"

He laid his hands on her shoulders, gripping her hard, full comprehension coming to him. "Dan Saxon knew that, too?"

"Yes. I told him. Perhaps I didn't need to. Dad is a hard one to fool."

He was suddenly completely sober, and coldness dwelt in the pit of his stomach. He said, "His own hand isn't much more than healed. The damn fool! Doesn't he know Telford will be expecting one of us to come rampaging?" He released her and started for the door.

Rita cried, "Where are you going?"

"After him!" he flung back. "Where else?"

Chapter Fifteen: THOSE WHO WAITED

AT LAMPLIGHTING HOUR OF THIS NIGHT, Cora Dufrayne sat waiting in her room in the Bagdad, a woman cold with anger and shadowed by her own dark thinking. She'd had a day of this, a day of bitter realization in which temper had burned itself out to a black ember that lay within her, hard and compelling. Last night a man of small account had made whisky talk; and because of this, Cora had learned to hate another man with harsh intensity, but out of the turmoil of that hate had come the realization that she hated herself even more. She was a straightforward woman, and she faced this now, knowing that today had been only the culmination of many days in which she'd groped toward a truth.

She had that sense of being tainted that had been hers since the day she'd bargained with Gault Telford. Sometimes she'd supposed it was smothered, but it had been with her always, giving her no peace. Now she knew from what it was she'd felt like fleeing. But now she could only pace restlessly, and wait. When at last the knock came, she crossed over and opened the door; and Gault Telford stood there.

She said, "Come in," and was surprised at the evenness of her voice.

He moved into the room. Lamplight caught on the lenses of his thick glasses, masking his eyes; but his full lips held a fixed smile, and she knew him to be a pleased man. He said, "The bartender brought word you wanted to see me. What is it, Cora?"

She said, "You were slow enough about coming!"

"I've been out of town a couple of days. A little trip to the county seat; a little business with the sheriff. It is finished." She hadn't asked him to be seated, but he took a chair and sat down heavily. She supposed her anger must be showing, for he said then, "You're upset. Some trouble here last night?"

"Not the kind that cuts into the profits," she said

and drew in a deep breath and felt herself turn rigid. "One of your Jimsons got bold enough to come to the bar. The drunker he got, the more he talked. He was making a brag about what he and his brothers did to Reb Kittredge, how they beat Reb and heaved him into an alley at your orders."

Telford spread his hands. "You supposed we would kill him. It was neither the place nor the time. Such things must be done carefully, Cora; we want the law always on our side. In spite of my better judgment, I gave Kittredge a last chance to come into line. He turned it down, but I was prepared for that. The Jimsons did a good job on him. He'll be a slow man with a gun for quite a while."

Cora said in a low and terrible voice, "Wait! Your drunken thug also told something else. He claimed that Kittredge is now owner of Circle-S and has been since the day he went out there. He won the ranch from Saxon at cards."

This jolted Telford—she could see the impact of it—but he managed a shrug. "It's true."

Her flaming thought was that she had to keep hold of herself, she mustn't let temper garble her tongue. She said quietly, "Gault, you told me he'd gone out there because of the Saxon girl."

Telford smiled. "If each man has his weakness, the same holds true for each woman, including you. I needed your help. If you thought you'd been bested by another woman, you were more likely to provide that help. What have you got to complain about, Cora? You drove a hard bargain and I've played square with you. You've got your quarter ownership, and you didn't even have to lure him to town. But I'm grateful for your telling me that the Jimsons would help."

She said then in full fury, "Damn you! You tricked me into selling Kittredge out!"

Telford said soothingly, "Look, Cora, if he's my enemy, he's yours. Nothing that I own—the basin ranches, my holdings in town, this place—is safe as long as Kittredge is opposed to me. I've had to scheme, and I've schemed carefully. That's why I rode a hundred miles to see the sheriff. When Circle-S gets cattle to railhead, Kittredge is going to find that his money is impounded. The sheriff will take care of that by telegraph. And Kittredge will come roaring into town, looking for me. But I'll be ready for him, and so will the Jimsons. Don't you see? I shall merely be defending myself against attack. The law will be able to take no other viewpoint. And when the smoke has cleared away, we shall be forever safe from Reb Kittredge."

She said, "So you're setting a trap for him."

"Exactly."

"And you tell *me* this?"

"You're my partner," he said. "It is plain to me that you harbor some sort of feeling for Reb Kittredge, but I'll wager that you love a quarter interest in the Bagdad even more." He stood up and turned toward the door; he paused there, the corners of his full lips quirking. "Isn't it about time for your first song of the evening?"

He was gone then, and she stood looking at the door he'd closed and was weak with a bitterer realization than any she'd known. She thought, *He supposes I'm like him, exactly like him,* and the old feeling of being tainted grew strong.

But she knew that Telford had felt free to tell her of his plans for another reason as well. He knew her helplessness and so had found a feline pleasure in this session. Kittredge was somewhere in the hills, far beyond reach. She had no way of getting to him, so Kittredge would ride blindly into Sleeping Cat and the trap that would be sprung. A shouted warning at the last moment? It would be too late then. A gun to back Kittredge? She had no skill with guns.

From downstairs the bedlam of the Bagdad rose; she was dimly aware that the piano signaled her to come to the tiny stage. She moved woodenly to the head of the stairs and got a glimpse of the packed barroom. Below were the scores of men who came nightly to hear her sing, and in this moment she needed one friend among them and realized that she had none. That was what a quarter interest in the Bagdad was worth! But in her turmoil, one thought compelled her. If there were a man to back Reb Kittredge at the showdown, he'd have a fighting chance.

Then she remembered the one friend she had in Sleeping Cat. She ran back into her room and got her cloak and came hurrying down the stairs, flinging the cloak over her shoulders. She turned at the bottom of the stairs and used the back door, letting herself out of the Bagdad. She groped in the alley's darkness and at last gained the street and sped along, oblivious to the startled stares of townsmen she brushed against. And in this manner she reached the cottage of Dr. Farrell, but the sight of it wrung a sob from her, for the cottage stood dark.

She'd seen Farrell often since that night they'd delivered the Walker baby. He had made it his custom to stop in at the Bagdad for a few minutes, whenever his duties permitted. He usually talked of his work, and she tried desperately to recall where he might be tonight. Then she hurried to the door and pounded upon it, her forlorn hope being that he'd come home from a hard day and gone to bed early.

She pounded until her fist hurt and she sank exhausted to the porch's planking, sick with the knowledge that not even Farrell could be reached in this hour when she most needed him. . . .

The Langstroms ranched along the eastern hills, to the south of Sleeping Cat, and Christopher Farrell had spent the night at the bedside of their daughter. She was fourteen, and he'd been watching her closely these last few days, for she'd shown symptoms of typhoid. Farrell had feared that most dread of frontier epidemics but drawn optimism from the thought that typhoid was difficult to diagnose. He could only continue his observations until the truth was known, but he'd now reached the conclusion that she was suffering from summer complaint. Thus he drove toward Sleeping Cat in the first daylight, a satisfied man and a tired one.

He came into the main street as the town was just stirring awake; he put up his buggy at the livery and walked back to his cottage. Birds chirped in the cottonwoods, and the air held freshness, and Farrell thought, *A fine time for a man to be going to bed!* Then he opened his own gate and swung up the walk; and when he stepped upon the porch, he saw the huddled figure near the door.

He was so tired that his eyes didn't at once focus, and his first thought was that some drunk had staggered here and fallen asleep. Then he recognized Cora's blue cloak. When he bent and touched her shoulder, her eyes opened and she looked at him wildly, then cast a startled glance about her. She said, "I kept waiting. I must have fallen asleep. Why, it's morning!"

"Come inside," he said, helping her to a stand.

She let him usher her into the house; she showed a readiness to talk. He could see how agitated she was, and his curiosity was great, but he said in his professional voice, "Some coffee first. Now sit down and do as the doctor tells you."

He installed her in one of the plush chairs and went to the kitchen and got a fire going and the coffeepot on. He was so sleepy that Cora's being here was like a dream. When he fetched in the coffee, she was staring blankly, her face pallid and drawn. She smiled a wan smile of thanks as he set cup and saucer before her.

"Now tell me," he said.

She told it all, from that first night when Kittredge had come to her and she'd proposed a partnership with him. She told of Telford's trickery and the bargain she'd made with Telford, and she didn't spare herself in the telling. She told of the drunken

Jimson who'd talked neither wisely nor well at the bar. She spoke of how she'd then sent for Telford and what Telford proposed to do and how she'd turned then in desperation to the door of this house.

Her voice droned on; and when she had finished her account, she lifted her eyes to him. "You see," she said, "there was no one else I could come to."

Whatever he had expected to hear, it had not been such a tale as this. He set down his own coffee, cold and untasted, and looked at his hands. "Kittredge means a great deal to you, I see."

"No," she said in that straightforward manner of hers. "He means no more than any other human. Once I thought he did, but now I know better. It's myself I'm trying to save. I don't want to spend all the rest of my life remembering that I betrayed him to his death."

Again he had that feeling that all this was a dream. "And what am I to do?" he asked.

"Stand by him when the time comes. It will come today, I think."

He began to laugh, his laughter low and ironic. She was sitting in the very chair Dan Saxon had occupied that night not so long ago. She was sitting next to the table where the letter lay that had come from Idaho. He said, "You want *me* to back Kittredge at the showdown?"

"Please, Chris," she said. "For my sake."

"I don't even own a gun."

"You can get one."

"I'll do whatever I can," he promised.

She stood up. "I'm going back to the Bagdad. All

that's left for me is the waiting."

"I'll come to you when I can," he said.

He let her out the front door and began an agitated pacing. He was woefully tired; his tiredness rose and clouded his thinking, and at last he stretched himself upon a couch. He dozed fitfully; even his sleep was pervaded with a grim consciousness of that to which he had pledged himself. He who had shied from violence had committed himself to violence, and that made for an irony beyond irony. But not even in sleep could he run from the reality of it, and so he tossed and turned and at last fell into a slumber of exhaustion.

He awakened with sunlight in his eyes and bestirred himself and discovered that it was already midafternoon. He got up then, moving like a sleepwalker. He felt hungry, but there was a squeamishness in him that warned him not to eat. He had some coffee and was glad for the warmth of it in the pit of his stomach. He got his hat and walked down to the mercantile and accosted Barney Shay behind his counter.

"I want a revolver," Farrell said.

Shay let his glasses slip to the end of his nose. "How's that?"

"I want a revolver," Farrell repeated sharply.

"Thirty-eight or forty-five?"

"How should I know? The bigger the better, I suppose."

Shay got a weapon from stock and laid it on the counter. "Here you are. Peacemaker model. Single action. Forty-five caliber. I can get you a carved handle for seven dollars extra."

"Never mind the handle," Farrell said. "Load this gun."

Shay obeyed, and Farrell paid for the gun and was conscious of Shay's eyes on his back as he walked from the store. The Colt felt very big in his hand, and very heavy; he tried shoving it into a pocket and found that it fitted none. He looked about; Sleeping Cat's street lay peaceful in the sunlight, only a few people showing on the boardwalks. He looked to the west from whence Kittredge would come riding. He wondered what to do next; this whole business was so beyond any experience of his that he felt empty-headed.

He began pacing the street, feeling ridiculously self-conscious with over two pounds of gun in his hand. He came upon an empty shack set down in the middle of the main street; it had been an earlier location of the saddle shop, which had since moved to larger quarters. The front of the shack was boarded up, but when he was moved by impulse to go around to the back, he found that the rear door gave to his hand. He stepped into the musty emptiness; dirt and debris lay upon rotting flooring, and cobwebs festooned the corners. Sunlight spilled between the boards covering the front windows and put a striped pattern upon the floor. The smell of leather still lingered.

He moved to the front and peered out. There were two or three inches between the boards, and he got a limited view of the street. He was west of Telford's office, and he thought, *Kittredge will have to pass this way*. This, then, should be as good a place as any to be posted to back Kittredge when the trouble started. He supposed there was nothing left now but the long waiting; he remembered Cora, who was also waiting; and he was suddenly proud to be here.

Then he was brought about by the scrape of a boot sole at the rear threshold, and he turned and felt that his legs were going to buckle under him. For one of the Jimson brothers was standing there.

This was Pete, the smallest of the three, the one who'd giggled and proposed to strip Cora that day of the holdup, the one whose hand had been seared by Kittredge's ready gun. He blocked the doorway, a wide grin on his face, and he said, "I just got mighty curious, Doc. Why you been pussyfooting around with a gun in your fist? Kittredge a friend of yours, maybe?"

Farrell tried to speak, but no sound came.

Pete Jimson advanced a step farther into the room. "No need to get any skin rubbed off *your* nose, Doc. Just hand over that gun like a good little boy."

"No," Farrell said.

Pete Jimson had been pleasuring himself. Now his grin faded, and he took on a look of dark ugliness. "I'm not foolin', Doc."

"Neither am I," Farrell said.

Whereupon Jimson fell into a crouch, his shoulders hunching and his hand moving toward the holstered gun at his hip. Christopher Farrell understood that gesture; he understood it full well. And that was when he realized that for any man there had to be an end to running and an end to compromising; there had to be a moment when he faced this sort of reality and found himself either ready or wanting. He was held spellbound, and his decision didn't even seem to be of his own making. He remembered vaguely that he'd once been told that you merely pointed a Colt as you would point your finger, and then you eared back the hammer and pulled the trigger. He did these things.

The explosion filled this tiny room and seemed to rock its walls; and a look of utter astonishment spread over Pete Jimson's face. The man was spun about by the impact of the slug; his legs went out from under him. Farrell came forward and stood over him and saw the widening bloodstain on Jimson's right coat sleeve, near the shoulder. He was conscious that boots pounded along the boardwalk and startled questions were being shouted out yonder on the street, but no one had oriented the shot, for soon the town quieted again. And all this while Farrell looked down at the unconscious figure of Pete Jimson.

Then he bent and took Jimson's pulse. It was strong enough. He laid the six-shooter upon the dusty floor and got out his jackknife and began cutting away Jimson's coat; and when he'd exposed the wound, he saw that it was not a bad one, though Jimson was losing blood. From his own handkerchief, Farrell fashioned a pad; and as he worked at fixing this in place, he suddenly knew why he had always shied from violence. His talent was at repairing the damage done by the violent ones. He had finished the bandaging when Jimson opened his eyes.

Jimson said, "For Gawd's sake, Doc, you won't let me bleed to death! Take care of me, Doc!"

Fear showed in Jimson's eyes and built a rind of sweat across his forehead, a greater fear than any Christopher Farrell had ever felt, an abject, crawling sort of cowardice that put contempt in Farrell. And witnessing this, he was freed from his own fears. He had shed a measure of them when he'd made his choice and raised the gun; he knew now that all along he had been a better man than Pete Jimson.

"I'll take care of you," he said.

But Pete Jimson had fainted again. Farrell stood up, thinking that now he must contrive to move the man. He looked toward the front of the building and at that moment he glimpsed someone riding up the street. His thought was, *Kittredge!* and he hurried forward for a better look. Then, peering between the boards, he sighed in relief; for it was Dan Saxon who'd come riding into Sleeping Cat.

Chapter Sixteen: GUN SMOKE IN SLEEPING CAT

KITTREDGE had left his horse tied before the telegraph shack in the railroad construction camp; and when he got the mount and rode out to the herd, a man sobered by sorry news, he found only Pecos and the cook. These two were holding the herd while the rest of the crew had gone into camp to eat and watch the fascinating business of a railroad spur being built. To Pecos, Kittredge said, a grim urgency in his voice, "Look over the *remuda* and cut me out the fastest horse that packs Circle-S's brand. And see how quick you can throw a saddle on him!"

Pecos squinted. "Dan got the best cayuse over an hour ago. You'll have to take second best."

"Then get leather on it!"

Pecos said with an old man's fretfulness, "Now why is everybody in such an all-fired rush? First Dan, now you."

"Rita can tell you about it," Kittredge said impatiently. "I've got to get riding. Cook, throw a little grub into a saddlebag."

The cook said, "What the hell is this supposed to be? A pony express relay station?"

But Kittredge was already trailing after Pecos, who'd got down off the chuck-wagon seat and gone to do as he was told. Kittredge helped with the saddling, after Pecos had found him a leggy roan that looked as though it might be both fast and long on bottom. Kittredge, clumsy with the kak, made no effort to hide his awkwardness. Pecos knew his secret anyway, and the time for pretense had passed. This was the time for action. There was the remembrance of Rita's agitated face as she'd told him about her father in the camp saloon. Now why in hell had Dan Saxon, that most careful of men, gone off half-cocked?

Kittredge lifted himself to leather, rode over to the chuck wagon and picked up the saddlebag the cook had prepared, waved his hand at Pecos, and lined out for the timber. He had one last look over his shoulder at the panorama of the construction camp.

And then he began the hardest ride of his life.

For the first few miles, backtracking over the trail the herd had taken, he rode as recklessly as the terrain permitted. His only thought was, *Faster! Faster!* Time and again he risked himself and the horse on rocky slopes, heedless of anything but the need to lop off the miles.

He didn't look for Saxon's sign. He gambled that Saxon would follow the hill trail down to Circle-S, then strike overland for Sleeping Cat. He tried to remember exactly how far it was to Circle-S; he recalled each day of the drive and the campfire talk when the crew had estimated how much ground had been covered. Five miles some days, ten miles at the best. He decided that it must be between thirty and forty miles to the ranch and, squinting at the sun, he wondered if he could make it to Circle-S before deep dark. After the first hour, he realized how futile was such a hope. There were too many places where the horse had to pick its way through brush and shale and deadfall.

But always he pushed onward and downward, growing angry when the pace had to be slow. Sky and timber and rocky trail became an endlessness never changing; he had the feeling that he rode a treadmill, taking toll of himself and the horse, getting nowhere. When he got occasional glimpses of the basin below, tawniness showing through the timber, he was tempted to find his own trail, remembering the short cut Rita had taken on the way up. But his only real knowledge of the hill country was over the route the herd had followed. He fought down his impatience, knowing that any deviation from the route might only slow him.

Sometimes he saw landmarks remembered from the drive—a lightning-blasted pine tree, a rock shaped like a beaver's head, a grassy meadow where the coosie had hauled his chuck wagon to a stop and doled out coffee. These were cheering sights; they made milestones of a sort and lessened the feeling that he was treadmilling. But when the sun dropped behind the hills, he realized that time was slipping away. After the brief twilight, he had to slow to a walk, even on the levels, for darkness claimed all the country. He rode with an elbow crooked before his face, wary of branches. Riding thus, he blundered upon Pecos's discarded wagon. This brought him a remembrance of that pain-wracked ride to Circle-S; this brought him also an acute reminder of his clumsy arm.

For an hour and another he groped his way along, and then he faced the inevitable. He'd better stop for the night. In one of those grassy meadows where a mountain creek brawled, he stripped gear from the horse and led the mount back and forth, gradually cooling it off and permitting it to drink sparingly. After that he improvised a squaw hobble from a gunny sack he'd picked up along the trail, ate the food from the saddlebag, and stretched himself on the blanket to sleep.

His thoughts ran riot; and when he half slumbered, he had the sensation of being back in the saddle and riding hard. He recognized this as a sign of tension and fatigue and was concerned; he would need to be a ready man when he reached Sleeping Cat. In his wakeful moments he shaped up cigarette after cigarette and lay with his head pillowed on his clasped hands, looking at the sky above and hoping that Dan Saxon, likewise, had decided to quit riding till dawn. He wondered where in the darkness and the hills Saxon was bedded. A mile away? Five miles? Ten?

He tried to understand what had driven Saxon and thought he found the answer. For Saxon, today had been like that first day, the day Saxon had challenged him in Sleeping Cat. Saxon played all his cards carefully, but there came those reckless moments when a last chip had to be tossed upon the table. Telford's trickery had made another such moment. Saxon had reasoned as he, Kittredge, had reasoned in the construction camp saloon. There was only one answer to Telford. But the thing that was still beyond Kittredge's understanding and stood now between him and sleep was the constant question—why had Saxon elected himself to fight Circle-S's fight?

He turned this over in his mind until exhaustion claimed him. He was up with the first show of light and into the saddle again, tightening his belt. In his mouth was the aftertaste of construction camp whisky, and he had a nagging headache. He wished he'd got more grub from the coosie, but he set his mind against hunger and pushed the horse hard. He knew that if Saxon hadn't stopped last night he might be almost to Sleeping Cat by now, and this made Kittredge reckless again. He rode the horse until the animal began to heave under him. Realizing that he must ration the horse's strength for all the miles that remained, he gave the mount respite.

The sun was not very high when he came to the meadow where Circle-S had made its camp the first night of the drive. Jubilation rose in him as he rode into this openness; now the worst of the terrain was behind him. After that, he looked for the place where the game trail he and Rita had taken rejoined the old logging road, but he couldn't be sure. From the promontories he saw a jungle of pine tops, and the sight of all that timber told him he'd best stay with the road.

In the midmorning he reached the bottom of the slope and could now skirt the hills on level ground to Circle-S. He lifted his flagging horse to a high gallop and held it there; he gritted his teeth against the punishment of the saddle, and shortly before noon he rode into Circle-S's empty yard.

Smoke lifted from the cookshack, and at Kittredge's shout one of the cowhands who'd stayed behind to guard the roundup gather showed himself.

"Dan Saxon here?"

"Changed horses and rode toward town about twenty minutes ago."

Relief left Kittredge weak. So Saxon hadn't pushed on through the night! Kittredge came down from the saddle and almost fell, knowing again that sensation that the earth was buckling under him. He looked at the sweat-and-foam-mottled horse that

had served him and was sorry for the horse, sorry
he'd had to ask so much of it.

"Saddle me the fastest hide in the corral," he
ordered. "And lead this cayuse till he cools off."

While the man went to do his bidding, Kittredge
lurched toward the cookshack. He should be making
the minutes count, but he had to eat if he was to
stick a saddle to Sleeping Cat. He came inside to
find the huge coffeepot simmering on the stove;
the aroma of that coffee seemed to Kittredge the
sweetest thing on earth. There was food in a frying-
pan shoved back from the heat—the dinner of the
man who was now taking care of the horse. This
food Kittredge wolfed down and followed with two
cups of coffee, strong and black. He even stole time
for the luxury of a cigarette, and then he came out
of the cookshack.

The Circle-S hand was still leading the spent horse
back and forth, and a saddled horse stood ready.
Kittredge hauled himself into the saddle, using his
right hand on the horn. Mounted, he realized that
though old habit had dictated his move, his arm
hadn't failed him. His arm was still stiff, but it had
supported his weight.

"I ate your dinner," he shouted at the Circle-S
man. "I'll cook you one when I get back."

Then he was away again, a fresh horse under him
and food in his belly and a feeling running through
him that he could lick the world. He discovered his
headache was gone. He was upon familiar terrain,
but he had to remember that Saxon was now nearly
an hour ahead of him. His first exuberance wore off,

fretful impatience returning. He resented the gates that had to be opened; but, true to rangeland tradition, he carefully closed them. Soon he was beyond Circle-S's acreage and lining out for Sleeping Cat.

Plying quirt and spur, he thundered along, the land blurring beneath him and the breeze of his own making a hard hand against him. He peered ahead, trying to sight Saxon's dust, but there was just enough rise and fall to the land to limit visibility. In midafternoon, he sighted Sleeping Cat and thereafter kept his eyes on the town whenever he could, watching the scatteration of buildings grow within his vision. But Sleeping Cat's nearness was still an illusion made of high, thin air and strong sunshine, and it was late afternoon before he rode into the outskirts.

And that was when he heard the guns speak.

The sound came from somewhere up the street— one shot, and another on its heels, the false fronts catching the thunder and echoing it. In Kittredge then was one sickening thought. *Too late!*

He flogged the horse onward and came into the familiar main street; and the scene was as he'd anticipated, the two rows of buildings and the horses at hitchrails and the loiterers withdrawn at the smell of trouble to peep furtively from doorways. Before the hotel, he saw Dan Saxon standing in almost the precise spot he'd stood that evening he'd braced Kittredge. Saxon held a smoking gun in his hand, and across the way Gault Telford lay crumpled in the dust, a gun, fallen from his hand, before him.

Kittredge flung himself off his horse; the horse

went bolting. "Dan!" Kittredge called.

Saxon turned his head and looked at Kittredge, but Saxon's real attention was elsewhere. "Watch out, Reb!" he shouted.

A bullet drove at Kittredge, tugging at the brim of his sombrero. Instinctively he leaped sideward and crouched, his hand dropping to his holster. Another bullet kicked dust at his feet; his sluggish arm obeyed him and he got his gun into his hand. He was faster than he'd hoped. Only now did he realize how thorough a trap had been set, and he marveled that Saxon still lived. Even Telford had been armed today. At least two men were firing from the cover of Telford's office doorway—the Jimsons, Kittredge judged. But it was still another's bullets that had come so close to Kittredge, and he saw Curly Mather then.

Mather had come around the corner of the stage depot to stand under its eaves. His face showed, set and stubborn through his own gun smoke; his eyes held hard on Kittredge, hating Kittredge. This was the way Mather was when Kittredge hammered a shot at him and saw Mather double over and fall on his face. This happened too quickly for conscious thought; then Kittredge remembered Saxon saying of Curly Mather the morning Mather had deserted, "I'll know where to find him when the time comes."

How well Saxon had known! There was an inevitability here, the inevitability that Mather, rejecting Circle-S in his blind hate and jealousy, would go straight to Telford to cast his lot with the man.

Kittredge thought, *He knew! At the last he knew*

*about my gun arm, for Telford told him. That was
why he got bold enough.*

He was aware that Saxon's gun was beating, and
he saw Christopher Farrell come running along the
boardwalk, revolver in hand. This astonished Kittredge, but there was no time for the full impact of
surprise. Two of the Jimsons were bolting from
Telford's doorway, running a zigzag course along
the street to a hitchrail. Kittredge, who'd been
fooled once, was thinking, *Where's the third one?*
Saxon was shooting, and Farrell had dropped to one
knee and was steadying his six-shooter across his
crooked left arm. But the Jimsons got into saddles
and jerked frantically at tie ropes, and suddenly
Kittredge was sick of gun smoke, and he let his right
arm sag; he let the Jimsons gallop up the street.

He looked at Saxon and shouted, "Where's the
other Jimson?"

Farrell stood up and said very calmly, "I put him
out of business."

"It's over, then," Kittredge said and was glad.

Walking to Telford's sprawled body, he looked
down at Telford and knew for a moment a surging
resentment against Dan Saxon. Kittredge had hated
no man so much as he'd hated Gault Telford. Yet
his hate was only a couple of weeks old, and Saxon's
had been forged across many years. Remembering
this, he saw that this day and this hour had been
Saxon's due, and his resentment was gone.

Kneeling, he turned Telford over and explored
the man's pockets till he found Telford's wallet. He
looked at Saxon, who still stood unmoving, for all

the world like an actor waiting his curtain call.

Kittredge said, "The notes are here. He didn't even bother to change the dates. He just told his lie to the sheriff and made it stick."

Saxon said woodenly, "They'd set a pat trap, but I'm guessing it was you they set it for. When I turned up instead, they were thrown off guard; and Telford made the mistake of showing himself when I shouted for him. I laid my tongue on him, goaded him into drawing first, just as I goaded you that night. You see, I've learned a bit about trickery myself. I downed him just as you came riding in. The others started shooting then."

Kittredge looked toward the far end of the street where settling dust marked the passage of the Jimsons out of Sleeping Cat. "They'll make a far campfire before they dare bed down," he predicted. "I'll bet they'll never show their faces on this range again." He came toward Saxon and stood before the man. Saxon smiled a slow smile and let the gun slip from his fingers, then pitched forward into Kittredge's arms.

Catching him, Kittredge cried, "You're hit! Farrell, give me a hand!"

"My shoulder," Saxon said. "I've lost blood, but I'm not badly hurt. I'll be all right."

Farrell was now at Saxon's side, showing a concerned face. "We'll get him down to my house."

They led Saxon along, supporting him. The street stood empty, no townsman yet showing himself; a shuddering silence held after the thunder of the guns. They got to the picket fence around Farrell's place, and Farrell said, "I can handle him the rest of the way. I'll bed him down for the night. He can go home tomorrow."

Kittredge said, "Take care of him, Doc." He looked at Farrell and saw a man transformed by this day's doings. He said, "You were a help when the smoke was thickest. It was that one extra gun that took the fight out of the Jimsons. What made you buy in, Doc?"

"Cora," Farrell said.

Kittredge turned thoughtful. "Then I'll go and thank her," he said. He looked at Saxon. "Sure you're all right?"

Saxon nodded.

Kittredge hesitated a moment. "Just one thing. I've got to know why you did it."

Saxon said, "I thought you knew. You were told once that the Saxons don't cheat. You had a clear ranch coming to you. That made it my chore. Now do you understand?"

"Yes," Kittredge said. "Everything."

Chapter Seventeen: A MAN'S IRON

KITTREDGE'S FIRST JOB was to catch up his horse. He found the mount in a weedy back lot and spoke soothing words to it, then led the horse to the Bagdad's hitchrail and tied it fast. Kittredge shouldered inside, only then remembering that this was Telford's place and here were Telford's hirelings. The silence brought him a sharp wariness. The bartender was an unmoving figure behind the mahogany; the few housemen sat hunched at their gaming-tables; the half dozen patrons at this afternoon hour were a hushed bunch. Only a percentage girl made a sound; she sat at a table, laughing softly.

Kittredge walked to the center of the barroom and canted his head in the direction of the street. "Some of you better go out there and move your boss."

The barkeep said, "We'll take care of it," showing no more emotion than if he'd been asked to hoist a barrel of whisky. Kittredge remembered the Jimsons, and it was his thought that some men lost their loyalty once the paymaster was no longer around. He climbed the stairs, putting his back to those in the barroom; and finding Cora's door open, he stepped inside.

She was seated by the window, her cloak over her shoulders. She looked old and burdened, like one recuperating from a long illness. She turned her head as he entered, and for a moment fright stood in her eyes. "Reb!" she cried.

"Telford's dead," he said.

"I know. I watched the whole thing from the window. He's fallen, and his house of cards will come crashing now. I'm not sorry."

He saw that she'd come through an ordeal that had been almost beyond bearing. He said gently, "I talked to Doc Farrell. He says you put him on my side. I've come to thank you for that."

"No!" she cried. "You owe me nothing. I sold you out, Reb. I'm the one who told Telford to fetch in the Jimsons. That got to be a hard thing to live with. In the end, I asked Christopher to square up for me."

He thought this over; and because the fists of the Jimsons had left an ache in his muscles, he was angry for a moment. But he finally said, "The thing I'll keep remembering is that you sent me help."

This quickened her, bringing a warmth to her eyes. "And now, Reb?"

He shrugged. "Somewhere I've traded trails. You asked me once if a woman could fit into my plans. I've found such a woman, Cora."

"I know," she said. "I've seen her. She'll be good for you, Reb. Better than I could ever have been. We're alike, you and I; but we're alike in badness as well as goodness. Together, nothing would have changed for us. Not long ago I helped Christopher deliver a baby. That baby has been named after me. You see, I found a man who showed me how useful I could be. I hear his footsteps on the stairs now. Yes, I've got so I know him that well."

Farrell showed in the doorway. He stood there, tall and slender, then walked inside in the manner of one who'd found himself any man's equal. He nodded at Kittredge and smiled. "Dan's doing fine. I've got him dozing in my bed. Coming here, I stopped by to look in on another patient. Pete Jimson. He's doing well, also. Well enough to have piled himself on a horse and stirred the dust out of here."

Kittredge said, "Twice I treated you rough, Doc. I hope you'll forget it."

Farrell said, "I was just as mistaken about you. I've found out some ills are for me to cure, some need your kind of treatment. You did Sleeping Cat Basin a great service today, the kind I couldn't have done alone. And I can leave now without feeling that I'm running."

"Leave?" Cora echoed, and was a stricken woman.

Farrell turned his eyes toward her and at once softened, his voice turning gentle. "I've come here to ask something of you, Cora. Something very important."

Kittredge made a move toward the door. "I'll be getting along."

"That's not necessary," Farrell said. "What I've got to say is for my friends to know." He looked at Cora again. "I shall be leaving for the Coeur d'Alene country soon. I'll be busy for a while establishing a practice over there, but that will serve to allow a decent interval to elapse. Then I want you to come and be my wife."

She was greatly moved; she looked close to crying. Kittredge saw her struggle to get hold of herself. She lifted her face and was never so handsome as at this moment. "I'd be proud, Christopher," she said, "but I think you'd come to regret such a marriage. You know what kind of road I've traveled; you'd keep remembering that. When I was a child, my people ranched along the San Saba. The Comanches came. I saw my mother violated and scalped. I saw my father put to a slow death. From that day, nothing ever mattered very much to me. There are things I've been that can't be changed now."

Farrell said, "You don't understand. I am the one who needs *you*. I've been only half a man. All that had to be brought out in me was brought out by you. The Coeur d'Alene is a hard country. I shall want you with me lest I ever falter. I think we shall be too busy looking ahead to look behind."

Cora said quietly, "Then I shall come when you send for me."

Farrell took a step toward her, and it was Kittredge's thought that neither of them now knew he was in the room. He left quietly and came down the stairs.

He was heading toward the batwings when the bartender said, "Have a drink on the house." He said this in an agreeable voice; and Kittredge turned to the bar, not really wanting the whisky. The bartender pushed a glass toward him and filled it and said, "We got that little job done out on the street."

Kittredge said, "He was your boss. But he asked for trouble, and he got it."

The bartender shrugged, his face emotionless. "He rode pretty roughshod over everybody. You don't see me crying. Those that ride rough are likely to end up in a heap."

"True words, friend," Kittredge said.

He was a solemn man then, with a last lesson learned. Odd that Telford should be the one to have taught it. He downed the whisky and felt its warmth and was relaxed. He looked at his own gaunt, saturnine face in the bar mirror and said aloud, softly, "You'd be a fair specimen of the handiwork of God if you'd shave your ugly mug."

He raised his hand in salute to the bartender and walked from the Bagdad and lifted himself to his saddle. He thought, *One more ride to make,* and headed westward.

Light glowed in Circle-S's ranch-house windows when Kittredge rode into the yard; and this surprised him, for the hour was late. He'd taken a slow way home from Sleeping Cat, sparing himself and sparing the horse; for all the accumulated hours and miles had weighed heavily upon him. He'd done much thinking on this return journey; he'd grown weary of thinking. When he saw the light, he supposed that one of the Circle-S hands who'd been left here was in the house. That one whose dinner he'd eaten, probably.

He rode to the corral and dismounted and began hauling gear from the horse. He was at this when a lantern bobbed across the yard as someone came from the house toward him. It was Rita; and this, too, surprised him. He'd left Rita up in the hills.

She held the lantern high and looked at him. She said, "I rode down as fast as I could. I knew that if either of you was able to come back, you'd come here."

He saw how very tired she looked; yet she was composed; she was ready for all the inevitabilities. Knowing this, he sought quick words to spare her the question she hadn't yet asked.

"Your dad got scratched," he said. "He's resting at Doc Farrell's. He'll be home tomorrow. Gault Telford's dead. I have the notes, and we can collect as soon as I show the railroad contractor that Telford was lying." He paused. "Curly's dead, too. He bought in on Telford's side."

He wasn't sure how she would take this last news. It hit her; he could see that. The lantern jiggled in her hand, but when she did speak, her voice was even. "He was a suspicious man," she said. "All of our lives it would have been the same—his spying on every move I made and twisting what he saw to his own imaginings. I was sorry for him when he was alive. I am sorry that he is dead."

Kittredge finished with the horse, forked hay into the corral, and walked back toward the ranch house. Rita came along with him, the lantern in her hand and their shadows scissoring in its light. She climbed to the gallery, but here he lagged behind.

From the foot of the steps, he said, "I'll be sleeping in the bunkhouse."

She placed the lantern on the porch and seated herself on the top step, drawing her knees up under her chin and folding her arms about her knees. "Just for tonight?" she asked.

"From here on out, Rita. The house belongs to Dan Saxon, who built it. So does the ranch. I'll talk to him when he gets back. I've got a little money in Denver. Maybe he'd let me buy into this ranch. I think we'd make a good pair of partners. We work pretty well together."

She shook her head. "The Saxons pay their gambling-debts. What about that?"

"I want only what I've really won," he said.

She drew in a quick breath; her face was suddenly alive with expectancy. "I've seen you change," she said. "I didn't know you'd changed so much. Why, Reb?"

He seated himself on the lowest step. He was a quiet, somber man still wrestling with the truths that had come to him. "Remember, you said that some day someone would bring me to my knees?"

"Curly? At the end?"

"No. Dan Saxon."

Again she shook her head, her face half lamp-lighted, half shadowed, showing puzzlement. "I'm afraid I don't understand."

He said, "I told you once that I figured I was born too late, born into a rigged world where those who'd had the easy pickings years ago could keep a hard bit in the mouths of men like me. Then I got my chance at ownership. I sweated the first day I rode out here, and I should have learned from that what ownership meant—sweating and taking responsibility, like I had to take when my crew was low on grub. The sort of thing you understood when you dug down into your own purse to pay Barney Shay for bullets that were needed to protect Circle-S. But there was even more that I didn't savvy, the constant standing guard a man had to do to hold what had come to him, first against Indians and rustlers and then against Gault Telford. Dan Saxon tried to tell me about that, but I was too concerned with what Reb Kittredge wanted. I didn't hear him."

She said softly, "No man could have told you the things you had to learn for yourself."

He nodded. "No part of it was free, not for Dan Saxon or any other man. I know that now. He buried a wife in the Nations, and that was part of the price. He kept paying across all the years in one way or another. He was paying at the last, when he rode to Sleeping Cat to brace Telford. He did that because he wanted to hand Circle-S over to me clean. That was part of ownership, too, the part I was slowest to understand—the pride a man has to take in his own iron. Some day, when I've lived enough years and soaked enough of my sweat into this ground, I'll be able to feel that kind of pride. It would be an empty thing, just winning ownership by a cut of the cards."

"Yes," she said, "it would be. Just as it would have been an empty thing for me to stay here if the thought had ever struck you that my staying was only a cheap bargain." She was smiling. "That was what I was trying to tell you the other night in the hills. A woman has her kind of pride of ownership, too, Reb."

He sat silent for a long moment, thinking of the things said, the things unsaid. He remembered how it had been that first day he'd ridden on roundup and found a pride in an old skill. He flexed his right arm, then rubbed it. He supposed that arm might never have its old quickness. A legend would die, and he was glad of its passing. Being a legend had meant being lonely.

He thought of Pecos and the others; he thought of the cook's row of pies bearing Circle-S's brand. He thought how it had been to belong to the crew. He said then, "Do you think I can make a deal with Dan Saxon to buy in?"

She said, "I think that Dan Saxon would do anything in the world to keep you here. It may sound queer, but I think that from the very first it was Reb Kittredge he hoped to save, even more than he wanted to save the ranch. He was a wild one, my father, long, long ago." Her eyes touched him. "And what kind of deal have you got to offer me?"

He smiled. "At the end of a day's work, if I'm not too dead beat out, will the boss's beautiful daughter, maybe, go riding with me?"

She said, "Reb, you hopeless fool! Did you ever wonder what it was that Curly saw from the very first that made him hate you so much?"

He turned this over in his mind until its full meaning struck him; and when it did, he knew she was as near as the reach of his arms. But first he stood up and picked the lantern from the gallery. He walked into the yard with it, toward the watering-trough, bent low, and held the light close to the ground. He searched for many minutes, and finally he picked up an object and came back to the gallery with it. He showed Rita the flint arrowhead he'd once thrown away.

"Ah, yes," she said.

He walked to the shutter from which he'd removed the arrowhead and used his gun barrel to drive it back into place. He said, "That's to keep me reminded of what I learned from Dan Saxon."

He held open his arms then and crossed the short distance to Rita. She had come to her feet and was awaiting him, her face softly beautiful in the lantern light. He took her into his arms and held her close and began laughing, not with merriment but with the full taste of a freedom he had never known before. She laughed with him, sharing his joy; and their blended laughter made a great, good sound in the night.

DELL'S ACTION-PACKED WESTERNS

Selected Titles